CAERPHILLY
COUNTY BOROUGH COUNCIL
CYNGOR BWRDEISTREF SIROL
CAERFFILI

Please return / renew this item by the last date shown above
Dychwelwch / Adnewyddwch erbyn y dyddiad olaf y nodir yma

ALSO BY GEORGIA

The Billionaire Banker Series

Owned
42 Days
Besotted
Seduce Me
Love's Sacrifice

Masquerade

Pretty Wicked
(Novella)

Disfigured Love

Crystal Jake
(The EDEN Series)

Sexy Beast

Click on the link below to receive news of
my latest releases.
http://bit.ly/1oe9WdE

Wounded Beast

Published by Georgia Le Carre
Copyright © 2015 by Georgia Le Carre

ISBN: 9978-1-910575-18-5

You can discover more information about
Georgia Le Carre and future releases here.

https://www.facebook.com/georgia.lecarre
https://twitter.com/georgiaLeCarre
http://www.goodreads.com/GeorgiaLeCarre

This book is dedicated to these AMAZING
women:

Caryl Minton,
Elizabeth Burns &
SueBee of 'Bring Me An Alpha'

The call themselves beta readers, but I call
them
my indispensible secret weapons.

Contents

ONE

Dom

Memories ...
Why do you come back?
— Amit Singh, Poet

Sometimes you read a book or watch a movie and you get to that point in the story when everything is about to change forever. At this point the characters could escape and go on with their life as if nothing had happened. The moment when the hero or heroine stands in front of a closed door and decides whether to go in and face the unknown, or walk away. Once, I thought I stood at that door.

But in real life there is often more than one door.

If I hadn't called my accountant that morning, or if I had called him five minutes later when I was already in the one-way traffic system and it was impossible to turn

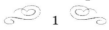

around and go back, I would never have come across that door. But I did call him, just before I reached the point where the traffic system would have made the door disappear.

'Hey, Dom,' he says briskly.

'What time is your appointment with the parasites today?'

'They're already at the restaurant. I'm driving there right now, but I'll probably be another twenty minutes. I hope they don't start talking to the staff or snooping around.' He sounds apprehensive.

'Where are you meeting them?' I ask.

'Lady Marmalade.'

'I'm less than five minutes away. I'll go and keep the fuckers company while they wait for you,' I offer.

'No!' he shouts suddenly, so loudly it makes my eardrum vibrate like a tuning fork.

'What the fuck, Nigel!' I swear, tearing the phone away from my ear.

He calms down double quick. 'Sorry, didn't mean to shout. But please, whatever you do, don't go there.'

'Why not?'

'It's just better.'

'You think I'm scared of those pug-ugly inspectors?'

'No, no, no, I don't think that at all. I'd just really appreciate it if you didn't confront them.'

'I'm not going to confront them. I'll just pass by and offer them a cappuccino.'

I hear him take a deep breath. 'Dom. In my professional capacity I have to advise you not to make contact with them. They're dangerous. Anything you say could lead them to deepen their investigation. I know how to handle them. You don't.'

'Look. I'm already turning in to the restaurant. Tell me their names. I'll be the perfect host, I promise.'

I hear him sigh dramatically. 'It's Mr. Robert Hunter and Miss Ella Savage.'

'A woman?' I ask surprised as I switch off the ignition, open the door and step into the light summer rain.

'You don't want to underestimate her. Savage by name and savage by nature,' Nigel cautions immediately. 'She's like the Snow Queen. Beautiful and ruthless. You definitely don't want to hit on her.'

I laugh. Nigel always amuses me. I own strip clubs full of beautiful, willing women with hardly any clothes on. I'm hardly desperate enough or foolish enough to try to chat up the tax officer who has come to break my balls. Although, I kinda like the idea of taking a snooty cow down a peg or two. 'Don't mistake me for Shane,' I tell him. My younger brother Shane is the playboy of the family.

'Look, all I'm saying is don't rock the boat in any way,' he urges in frustration.

The back door of the restaurant is open, and some of my staff are lounging around smoking cigarettes under the canopy.

3

'Morning, boss,' they greet cheerfully, and I raise a finger in acknowledgment.

'Hang on, Nigel,' I say into the receiver and turn toward my boys. 'Are the tax officers inside?'

They nod. 'Yes, boss. Maria has already offered them coffee. They looked a bit pissed off that there was no management here to meet them. The bloke's gone to the toilet— he's been in there for the last five minutes— and the woman's waiting in the restaurant.'

I thank them and step into the washing up area of the restaurant. The dishwashers are running and it is noisy. I wait until I get to the kitchen area before I put the phone back to my ear.

'Right, Nigel, I'll see you in about fifteen minutes.'

'I'd really prefer it if you did not meet them, Dom,' he says, barely able to mask his anxiety.

'I know. You said.'

'Whatever you do, don't antagonize them,' he pleads.

'I won't.'

'Right. Just remember: the less said, the better. Don't let her manipulate you into revealing anything.'

'There's nothing to reveal, Nigel,' I say and kill the connection.

I nod at my chef, Sebastiano. He's standing over a hunk of meat laid out on the stainless steel table. In his right hand he's holding a knife, and with his left hand he's

stroking the meat as if it's alive to locate the juiciest, most tender part so it can be precisely carved out and presented as tonight's Chef's Special. Cutting meat properly is a skill as old as hunting itself.

I walk past the fridges and the tables with the heating lamps suspended over them before reaching the swing door to the restaurant. Before I go in I stop and look through the round glass hole in the door. The restaurant is mostly in darkness. Only one section is lit. My eyes fall on the woman sitting under the light. At that moment she lifts her head from a file she is studying and I see her face.

FUCK! FUCK! FUCK!

I jerk away from the glass in shock and disbelief and lean against the cold tiles of the wall. Air is no longer reaching my lungs. My heart feels constricted, as if steel hands have reached inside my body and are squeezing it like a lump of fucking dough. I gasp for breath. How can fate be so fucking cruel to play such a trick on me? Why?

Something deep inside me starts screaming.

And suddenly, I'm not standing outside the door to my restaurant anymore. I'm in freezing, black water. All around me is pitch-dark. My legs are still kicking, but feebly. Far away in the distance I can see the headlights of the boat. Jake is coming.

I want to scream, but I can't.

My skin feels too fucking tight. Like the animal in the cage that chews at its own bloody tail in horror at its loss. In my peripheral vision, Sebastiano is holding the knife at the perfect angle as he slices into the muscle and fiber. That meat is dead. It will not feel the sharp steel cutting into it. I too am dead. I will not feel the pain.

Ah, it's that fucking door again. But I can walk away, and nothing in my life will change. I can remain dead.

I take a deep breath. I can still walk away. I should walk away.

But I don't.

I open the door and enter the restaurant.

And Ella Savage turns her head and stares coldly at me.

TWO

Ella

The first sensation I have at the sight of him is one of pure disquiet. Like stroking a cat against the lie of its fur. Something perfectly silky and smooth has become ruffled. It neither feels nor looks right.

My brain processes what my eyes see in disjointed bits.

Tall, broad, flat stomach, narrow hips. Serious swagger. Fit, but not gym fit: combat fit. A fighter. The long, prowling strides with which he is eating the distance between us give the impression of coiled tension. A slowly stalking animal about to spring on its prey.

As he moves out of the gloom, his face catches the light.

His hair is damp from the rain and longer than in the photographs I found on the net. It curls around the collar of his leather jacket. And his face is ruggedly beautiful with the kind of tense jaw and five o'clock shadow that must leave delicious burns on a woman's inner thighs. Whoa! Where the hell did that come from? I suck in a harsh breath. A word I hardly ever use pops into my mind: rideable.

Not a good word, Ella.

Not a good word.

Oozing aggression and male strut, he comes to a stop in front of the table I'm sitting at and stares down at me. The sheer height and breadth of him is so overpowering, it actually makes me feel oddly shaky. *What the hell is Rob still doing in the toilet?* My skin tingles. Masking my unease, I return the angry alpha's stare coolly.

The light is directly above him so I cannot be certain of the color of his eyes, but they are light, and as fierce and intense as an eagle's. His chin tilts a fraction higher, and I see the gleam of his irises between his hooded lids.

They are blue: hot blue.

As if the sun had shone onto the ocean's surface and made it sparkle with reflected light. The unblinking orbs work their way over my face, lingering on my mouth, then sliding down my neck, and coming to rest on my breasts. I take a shocked lungful of air at the blatant arrogance.

His lips twist cynically at the rise and fall of my chest.

 8

Even though I'm wearing my customary cotton shirt and a buttoned-up jacket, and only the suggestion of the shape underneath is on show, I flush deeply. His eyes sweep upward back to my scarlet face.

'Miss Savage, I presume,' he intones. His voice is deep and sexy. It feels like something warm melting down my back.

I straighten my spine and try to look unaffected. 'And you are?'

'Let's not play games, Miss Savage. You know exactly who I am.'

'I'm not playing games,' I reply calmly. 'I'm trained not to make assumptions.'

He doesn't smile. 'Except one?' His voice is acid.

I raise a coldly disdainful eyebrow. 'I beg your pardon?'

'You operate under the assumption that there is always an underlying intention to cheat.'

'If I'm involved there usually is.'

The shockingly blue eyes flash with temper, but his voice is tightly controlled. 'If you're implying what I think you are, Miss Savage ...'

I let the corners of my lips twitch upwards in a deliberately fake smile. 'If you have done nothing wrong then you have nothing to fear, Mr. Eden.'

'I wasn't aware I had anything to fear. I thought you were investigating the restaurant. I'm just an employee of the company that owns this restaurant.'

'Just an employee?' I repeat disbelievingly.

'Just an employee,' he insists softly.

I look at him steadily. 'In that case, you are not qualified to give me the information I require. Where is Mr. Broadstreet? This meeting is supposed to be with him.'

'Nigel has been delayed. Trust me when I say I *am* qualified to give you the information you require,' he informs, and begins to remove his leather jacket.

Underneath the blue shirt—*Is that silk? He definitely didn't get that off a store rack. It screams custom*—all kinds of eye-wateringly lovely muscles are rippling up and down his torso and upper arms. I watch him fit the jacket over the back of a chair and start rolling up his shirtsleeve. His forearm is brown, thick, and populated by silky, dark hairs.

My heart skips a beat; then begins to race. There is something incredibly erotic about being alone in an empty restaurant while a full-on, hundred percent certified alpha strips down under a pool of golden light. I catch my wandering thoughts and concentrate on the gold watch on his wrist. Of course, a Rolex. Just an employee, huh? A dishonest, lying, cheating dirtbag, more like.

He slides into the chair opposite me, and suddenly he is too damn close, the smell of his cologne punching me in the middle of my chest. The moment becomes charged. Somehow strangely filled with ... oh fuck ...

sexual tension! Last thing in the world I need. *Where the bloody hell is Rob?*

Feeling flustered and awkward, I drop my gaze to the file in front of me. I'm a tough cookie. I'm here to do a job. I'm here on behalf of the Queen and country.

Resisting the impulse to turn around and look for him and so betray my intense discomfort, I take a deep breath and meet Dominic Eden full on, at close quarters.

And Oh! My! God!

The sexiest man in the entire fucking world is staring straight at me with *hunger* in his eyes. My mouth falls open. His eyes zero in on my lips. The air around us becomes electrified.

Whoa! What the ...!

I want this man to fuck me raw right here on this table in the middle of this darkened restaurant. The sensation vibrates down my spine and ends in a dull ache between my legs. The intensity of my desire for him shocks me. Doing this job, I've gone to a lot of trouble to hide, and even deny my sexuality, but it has always been there, lying in wait. Waiting for the right man to awaken it.

Knowing that doesn't make my reaction or my unprofessional behavior any less embarrassing. I have to pull myself together. Dominic Eden cannot know how affected I am by him. Taking a deep breath I raise my eyes and look into his. It's like a zebra trying to outstare a lion.

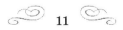

From the shadows comes the sound of a door opening. Someone is approaching us. I swallow hard unable to pull my eyes away from his, but before whoever it is can come up to our table, Dominic Eden breaks our stare, lifts his hand and holds his thumb and forefinger in the way that you would do if you wanted to show someone the measurement of an inch. I have been investigating restaurants long enough to know that the gesture means espresso, short.

The waitress goes away silently.

I cough. 'Er … When do you expect Mr. Broadstreet to join us?'

'Fifteen minutes or thereabouts,' he murmurs and nonchalantly leans forward. I can't help it I flinch back as if avoiding a bullet, my hands grasping the edge of the table, and my heart galloping madly.

At that moment the waitress comes back. I look up at her, grateful for the distraction. On her tray is not a small espresso but a small liquor glass of some colorless liquid. Neat alcohol for breakfast? Wow!

She puts the glass on the table and immediately slinks back into the dim of the unlit restaurant. He leans back, completely relaxed, his forearms resting on the table. His eyes never leaving me, he reaches for the glass and downs the liquid in one swallow. He places the glass back on the table and smiles, the smile of a shark.

Not a shark smiling at a human, but a shark smiling at another shark.

It's a 'come out and play' smile from one predator to another.

Freaked out by my unexpectedly strange and intense reaction to him, I clear my throat. 'Shall we ... um ... start?' I stammer. I desperately need to regain some control over this situation. In a strange reversal of roles we are reading from the wrong scripts. It is he who should be fearful and respectful, and it is I who should be playing the part with all the power and authority. I am the tax inspector. He is the tax cheat.

'By all means,' he says, his eyes plenty hostile.

'Look, Mr. Eden, we need to collaborate, work together on a cooperative, non-adversarial basis in order to resolve this situation.'

'Non-adversarial? Is there a way to diplomatically throw someone under a bus?'

'I'm not here to throw you under a bus.'

'No? Aren't you here to screw as much money as possible out of this company?' A cold menace is in his voice.

'No,' I say firmly.

'You'll be telling me next I can eat a shit sandwich and not have brown teeth,' he says rudely.

But I refuse to rise to the bait. I am too professional for that. 'We are here to

establish whether this restaurant is paying the correct amount of tax that is due.'

He hits the flats of his palms on the table and makes a hissing sound of disbelief. 'Do *you* even believe that bullshit?'

I jump, and for a millisecond I experience a sense of searing shame. He's absolutely right: I am here to squeeze every last drop of money possible. In fact, I wouldn't even be here if we had not already assessed that a substantial sum can be gleaned from this establishment. And the moment we find a flaw we'll be piling on interest charges and fines on top of any amount deemed to be owed to cover the cost of our involvement.

Then I remember my honest, hardworking parents. How proud they were that they paid their fair share even though all around them people were gaming the system. And yet now that they've both stopped working because my father is ill and my mother is his primary caregiver, their combined pensions are barely enough to get them through the month. And the reason there isn't enough is because of people like him. People who refuse to pay their fair share. Corrupt, devious people who get away with it just because they have expensive lawyers and accountants who arrange all kinds of sweet schemes for them.

Well, I took this job with Her Majesty's Revenue and Customs (HMRC) because I

believe in the good we do and I'm here to make the world a fairer place.

I meet his eyes head on. 'If it transpires that you've paid the correct amount of tax, we will not harass you in any way.'

Before he can answer, the restaurant door opens and Rob comes in. We turn to watch his progress across the room. As soon as the light hits him, I see that he looks a sickly shade of green. I raise my eyebrows enquiringly at him. He shakes his head imperceptibly at me, and turns toward Dominic Eden.

'Sorry about that. I think I've picked up some kind of stomach bug. Can we reschedule this meeting for another day?'

'Of course, Mr. Hunter,' Eden says. There's a taunting smile in his voice.

I gather up my files, stand, and take a couple of steps forward so Rob's body is between him and me. Eden unfurls himself and stands, towering over Rob and me. Rob extends his hand, but he refuses to shake it, and Rob retracts his hand awkwardly.

'Right,' Rob says. 'We'll be in touch to make another appointment.' He turns around and starts walking toward the door.

Eden turns to mc.

I nod and quickly follow Rob without looking back, even though I can feel Eden's stare like a dagger in my back. Rob holds open the door and I step out into the entrance foyer. My heart is racing. What happened in that empty restaurant was so

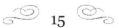

crazy and so unlike anything I have ever encountered that I can't even think straight.

I look at Rob as he enters the foyer and closes the door behind him. There's a pinched look about his mouth, and his chubby face is shiny with perspiration. I must admit he doesn't look too well.

'Rude cunt,' he mutters disgustedly.

My eyebrows shoot up. Rob is never so crude. He must be feeling really unwell—or Dominic Eden rubbed him up the wrong way.

'Are you all right?' I ask cautiously.

'No, I feel bloody awful, but I'll survive. I just need to get home. Will you drive?'

'Sure,' I say, opening the street door. Outside it is still raining steadily.

Rob turns toward me. 'Damn, I left my umbrella in the restaurant. Will you be good enough to get it for me?'

I look at him in dismay. 'Me?'

'I'd go myself, but I'm not well, Ella,' he says irritably.

I continue staring at him. I really don't want to go back into that restaurant alone.

'Can't you see that I'm suffering?' he asks through clenched teeth.

'Yes, yes, of course.'

'It's by the table. Hurry, please. I'm afraid I'll have to rush to the toilet again.'

Without a word I go back into the foyer and, after crossing the small space, open the door of the restaurant.

THREE

Ella

The first thing I see is the muscular bulk of Dominic Eden sitting at the table. He's hunched over with his forehead resting on his fist. At the sound of my entrance his head jerks up. His eyes are brimming with tears and the expression on his face is shocking.

He looks utterly tormented!

In fact, it appears to me that I have interrupted him in a moment of such extreme suffering that it seems impossible he is the same hostile, high-octane, sexual man I left a few minutes ago. This man could have just walked off a battlefield, the cries of the dying still ringing in his ears.

Horrified by the intensely private moment of grief I have accidentally stumbled upon, I begin to babble nonsense. 'I'm sorry, I didn't mean to ... Rob forgot his umbrella. I've come ...' My voice dies away at the change in his face.

It's an expression that is raw and primal and impossible for me to understand. The closest I could come to describing it is to say that it's almost a look of desperate yearning. As if I've taken something of great importance from him and he is silently begging me to return it, and yet ... how could it be?

We just met in antagonistic circumstances. I have not taken anything from him. Not yet, anyway. It doesn't make any sense.

Outside this closed, deserted restaurant, the world revolves inexorably: Rob waits with irritation, I have a two o'clock appointment I have to cancel, my mother will be cleaning the bathroom and waiting for my call to tell her what time I'm planning to pick her up tomorrow, my best friend Anna will have presented her dreaded sales report and be wanting to tell me all about it.

But in this strange world, I can do nothing except gaze at Dominic Eden in a daze. His suffering moves me more deeply than I care to admit and the part of me that I never allow out when I am at work, the part that gets angry when people are cruel to animals, propels me towards him. My hand reaches out and my finger lightly brushes his face. It is meant to be an expression of sympathy, but a small spark rushes up my arm.

The tax dodger and I stare at each other in shock.

We are connected at such a deep level it is even beyond attraction, desire or lust. I don't know how long I would have stood there if not for the expression of fury that suddenly crosses his face. He jerks away from my finger. The rejection is like a slap in the face.

He blinks away the tears, and I unlock my frozen muscles and force my hand down. I turn away from him blindly, my mind blank with shock. I'm here for Rob's black umbrella. I start looking around and spot it tucked under the table close to his leg. Yes, that's what I came for. I bend, grab it and quickly straighten.

'Well, I'll be off then,' I say awkwardly.

Without looking him in the eye again, I begin to hurry toward the door. I place my hand on the door handle and turn it.

'Will you have dinner with me, tonight?' His voice rings out and wraps around me like a cloak.

Dinner with him?

I take a deep breath. Oh my! It's shocking how much I want to agree. I turn around slowly. 'I'm sorry, I can't. It wouldn't be appropriate,' I say quietly.

'Why not?'

'You're under investigation and I'm the investigating officer. It would be wrong.'

'I thought it was the restaurant you were investigating.'

'You know it's the same thing,' I answer more truthfully than I normally would have done.

'Don't you think you'd find out more about me and the restaurant over dinner than you would pouring through dull reports from your central computer.' His voice is soft and persuasive.

Desire clings to my ankles like the waves that suck at your feet when you're standing at the shoreline. 'I don't think that would be very ethical.'

'Spare me the crap, Ella. They'll fucking hang a medal on you if you bring in a rope of information to hang me with.'

'Look, Mr. Eden—'

'Dom,' he corrects softly.

I bite my lower lip and hover uncertainly by the door. I have never been so confused or conflicted before. He gets to his feet and starts walking toward me. Instantly I feel a flare of panic. He comes within two feet of me before stopping. Too close. Way too close. His face is no longer in the light, but deeply shadowed, the outlines faint. Only his eyes shine with lust.

The damp curls caressing his powerful neck make me itch to push the fingers of both my hands into them. I even imagine myself sluttishly dragging my fingers up his scalp. As if he has heard my thoughts he leans closer. His scent invades my nostrils and my breath hitches. Staring up into his eyes, I feel my body slowly inching toward him. There is

 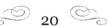

no doubt in my mind that he is dangerous for my sanity. That I should say no.

That I *must* say no.

'Will you come?' His deep voice seduces in the dark.

I really want to say no. I really, really do. It's the right thing to do. The most professional thing to do. But I remember again how we stared into each other's eyes and I felt as if our souls were touching.

And there is this attraction: irrational, crazy and unlike anything I have ever experienced. My mouth is watering to taste him and it is beyond words or explanations.

Am I just behaving in this reckless way because he's so drop-dead gorgeous? Or is it because I saw something I shouldn't have seen? Or is it because beyond my professional pride, my life is pretty dreary, and he is one of those shining things that come by once, if you're very lucky, in a lifetime?

Whatever it is, it makes me feel like an iron filing helpless in the pull of a giant magnet. This *thing* between us is unlike anything I have ever experienced and it is blatantly clear that I am not going to be able to think of anything but him for weeks. Either with regret that I succumbed to temptation, or with regret that I did not reach out and take what I wanted so badly. It is so hard to say no to someone your body craves, but say no I must.

Two throaty words tumble out. 'All right.'

'Good,' he mutters, and I'm startled to hear the same conflict in his voice that I heard in my head. He doesn't want to want me! It's just as inconvenient for him.

'I'll pick you up at seven?' he murmurs.

I nod.

'Where from?' he asks.

'7, Latimer Avenue.'

'Give me your phone,' he commands.

I hesitate a moment. Every brain cell that I have painstakingly trained over the many years to be independent, strong and take no bullshit from anyone cries out HELL NO, and every untrained, uninhibited, natural cell in my body screams FUCK YES.

It's just once in a lifetime.

I hand over my phone and watch him input his number into it and press call. A sound vibrates from his jacket. He ends the call and gives my phone back to me. The tips of our fingers graze and that brief, impersonal touch steals the wind from my lungs. The spark is undeniable. It lights up my body and makes my mind reel with images of us twisted together, our mouths fused, our sweaty bodies joined. I almost want to purr like a needy kitten. It's a far cry from the woman who strode into this restaurant like a consul less than an hour ago.

My fingers are tingling as I raise my eyes to search his. 'Why do you want to take me out to dinner?'

'Do you really want me to answer that?'

Our mouths are only a heartbeat away. I shake my head.

The answer is throbbing between us. I have never met a man I wanted the way I want him. But what shocks me is that a man like him should want me in the same way. Yes, I'm good-looking, but he has access to the most beautiful women.

Sex. Sex. Sex. And so what?

'Seven OK with you?'

'Yes.'

FOUR

Ella

I make it out of the restaurant and drive Rob back to his flat. Then I get back to the office and try hard to be interested in a piece of gossip the receptionist has for me. I smile and nod at my colleagues as they walk by. I go to my floor and get myself a mug of coffee. Sitting at my desk, I put away the file marked 'Dominic Eden', and call my mother. She's a terrible worrier, and she is quietly relieved to hear from me. I tell her I will pick her up at twelve tomorrow. With that arrangement made, I ask after my father.

My mother drops her voice to a whisper. 'I think he's feeling a bit down, love. His prostate is playing up. It keeps him awake at night.'

'Let's all do lunch tomorrow,' I suggest brightly.

She seems pleased with the idea.

24

Almost as soon as I ring off, Anna's call comes through. Even by the tone of her voice, I can tell that her meeting went badly.

'I think I'm going to be fired,' she wails.

'They'd be mad to fire you. You're the best salesperson they have,' I say reassuringly. And that's no lie, either. Anna can close a deal like no one else I know.

'I kinda fucked up, Ella. I slept with my sales manager.'

'What?' I exclaim, shocked. 'Tony's disgusting!'

'I was drunk,' she says glumly.

'Oh my God! And he's married as well.'

'Tell me something I don't know,' she says sourly.

'When did this happen?'

'Last Friday.'

'And you're just telling me now?'

'It meant nothing. I was, like, really drunk,' she explains.

'Oh, Anna.'

'I'd already put it behind me, but now he's acting all weird. I think he's trying to get rid of me.'

Note to self: NEVER mix business with pleasure. Oh, DAMN.

After my conversation with Anna, I have a salmon and cucumber sandwich and some dark chocolate for lunch. That afternoon I get through an impressive pile of paperwork, answer the phone, and liaise with my workmates, but all the time my insides

are clenched, and between my legs my cunt is fat with anticipation.

Before the clock strikes five, I am already crossing the reception concourse. Stepping outside into the hot evening, I walk down to the Underground station and take the Tube back to my apartment building. Ignoring the slow, smelly lift, I run up the three flights of stairs and let myself into my matchbox-sized, one bedroom flat. Yeah, it's tiny, but it's all mine—well, at least as long as I pay my rent.

I run to the mirror and look in it.

Unbelievable.

I still look the same. I pulled it off. No one knew.

My living room is west facing and it's like a sauna in my home, so I quickly open all the windows, switch on the fans and go into my bedroom. Even though it's very small, I've made it look pretty and cozy with blue and white vertical stripe wallpaper, an old-fashioned chrome bed and a painted French dressing table. It's my sanctuary. So far only one man has been in here, but he turned out to be a giant jerk. I quickly banish all thoughts of him and open more windows. The sounds from the street below float up as I start stripping the bed. I put on fresh sheets and stuff the soiled ones into the washing machine. I don't turn the machine on, because I don't want to come home to a crumpled wet mess.

I tidy up, dust all the surfaces and run the vacuum cleaner quickly around the place. By now I'm hot and sweaty. I glance at the clock: five past six. I stick a green apple scented refill into the plug-in air freshener and go into the bathroom. There I do what I've not done in months.

I trim down my bush and shave my legs. No nicks. Yay! I step into the shower and wash my hair. With a towel wrapped around my head and body, I come back into the bedroom and pad over to my closet.

It's been a long time since I cared this much about looking good. There are all kinds of options I can go for: sexy, or casual, or elegant, or professional. In the end I decide to go for subtle. A black lace shirt that my mother bought for my birthday teamed with a red pencil skirt that I got in a seventy percent off sale. I guess there's not too much demand for red pencil skirts. But the nice thing about the skirt is the slit up the back. Modest, but an invitation all the same.

You're not on a date, I tell myself even as I'm slipping into little bits of sexy underwear. Standing in my bra and panties, I dry my hair and, brushing it back, draw on a black velvet band. I go for smoky eyes and nude lip gloss. My cheeks are already tinged with pink so I skip the blusher.

From the back of my closet I take out my most extravagant purchase yet. I saved up for weeks to buy them. I open the box and take out my big investment: a pair of zebra

27

patterned court shoes with red heels almost the same color as my skirt. I step into them and … they are worth every penny.

Feeling like a million dollars, I dab on perfume and stand in front of the mirror on the closet door. I turn around and look at the back view.

'Not too bad,' I reassure myself.

I stuff my lip gloss, a twenty-pound note just in case it gets nasty and I need to get a taxi home, and a credit card into my evening purse. With one last look at my appearance, I go into the living room. It smells of apples. Satisfied that everything looks the way it should, I glance at the time.

I still have ten minutes to kill.

Until this moment all the activity has kept me going and in control. Now I'm suddenly a bundle of nerves. I feel as if I'm about to walk into an exam hall to take a test that I'm totally unprepared for. I walk into my kitchen and take a bottle of vodka out of my fridge. I pour two fingers worth of alcohol into a glass and down it neat into my empty stomach. It burns my throat, but the alcohol is good. Its warmth radiates quickly through me, warming my body, stirring my blood. I switch on the TV for some noise, and try to concentrate on the sounds and pictures on the screen.

The doorbell makes me jump like a startled cat at two minutes to seven.

The man is punctual!

28

I smooth my skirt and, taking a deep breath, open the door. And ... oh wow! If he looked good before, he is devastatingly dashing now in a snowy white silk shirt that contrasts amazingly with his tanned skin, a beautifully cut gunmetal gray evening suit, and black shoes polished to a mirror shine. Is that jaw for real? Freshly shaved, his jaw seems to me to have been chiseled to perfection by the gods themselves. As Anna would say, 'Gurllll! I'ma gonna have to call you back.'

'Hi,' I say awkwardly.

Silently, he holds out what looks like a box of very expensive, handmade chocolates. Wow, I certainly didn't expect that from a twenty-eight-year-old gypsy tax dodger. I take the box and finger the dark blue ribbon.

'How ... courtly. Thank you,' I say softly. My mother used to say any charm offensive that begins with handmade chocolates is bound to take effect eventually. I wonder when eventually will be.

He shrugs, his hot blue eyes pouring over me, taking in my face, my hairband, my lace top, my red skirt, and resting a shade longer on my zebra shoes.

He brings his eyes back to my face. 'Are you ready to go?'

'Yes,' I say, taking a step back to leave the box of chocolates on the little table by the door. I turn around to find his eyes scanning the interior of my tiny flat. When his gaze meets mine it is polite and deliberately neutral.

Stepping out, I close the door and we walk down the corridor to the lift without any conversation. He presses the button and still there are no words exchanged. His silence is unnerving, and I feel compelled to break it before the lift comes.

'Where are we going?'

He glances sideways at me. 'The Rubik's Cube.'

The lift doors open and we step in. The smell of piss hits me hard. 'The Rubik's Cube? It's not one of yours, is it?'

He looks at me sardonically. 'Take you to one of mine and have you accuse me of enjoying untaxed perks?'

'Right,' I say, as the lift slowly and jerkily bears us down.

His car, a model I recognize immediately as it's my father's dream car, is a brand new Maserati GranCabrio Sport bearing a price ticket of over a hundred thousand pounds. It's parked on double yellow lines right outside the building entrance.

'This road's notorious for parking tickets,' I warn, my eyes skimming the muscular lines of the sleek black machine.

'I know,' he says carelessly.

He unlocks the car remotely and opens the passenger door for me. I slip in and he shuts it. Alone in the luxurious space, I inhale deeply the smell of leather and

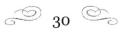

immerse myself in the high-tech beauty and fabulous comfort of the interior. I stroke the door handle. Wow! I've never been in such a car. The dashboard, door and seats are all in soft burgundy leather with stitching in a matching color.

He slides into the driver's seat, retracts the roof, pushes a little button next to the column marked 'Sport', and what must be the loudest car in the world snarls, roars and with a sonic boom comes to life.

He turns to me. 'Ready?'

'Should I be scared?'

'Nah, you'll love it.'

I'd planned to play it cool, but a wild, unintended whoop escapes my thick wall of disapproval of him and ill-gotten wealth of all kinds when he hits the gas pedal, and the car takes off so suddenly it throws me back against the seat.

When I first saw the roof disappearing from above my head, I did worry about what kind of mess my hair would be in by the time we arrived at the restaurant, but the car has been built in such a way that my hair remains impressively unruffled. And the V8 engine is so brilliantly noisy with pops and bangs on the overrun that there's no need for conversation at all as we speed down empty back roads.

The noise also means that we're constantly the center of attention everywhere we go. It's a lovely summer evening and people are sitting outside restaurants, pubs

and bars eating and drinking—so that makes for a lot of attention. And when we make a traffic light stop, excited tourists lift their phones and film the car.

He drives up to the Rubik's Cube's pillared entrance, gets out, and opens my door. Putting his hand lightly on the small of my back, he throws the keys to the parking jockey who catches them neatly. Even though his hand is barely touching me, I'm conscious of it as he guides me up the glossy granite steps. The imposing entrance has an air of intimidation about it, as if one runs the risk of being challenged by the staff with the question, 'Are you rich enough to be here?' The answer to which in my case is clearly no.

But apparently Dom is.

The doormen are impressively enthusiastic in their welcome, and it's instantly obvious that not only is he a regular here, but he must also be a tipper of massive proportions.

The restaurant is on the first floor, and we climb a sweeping, black-carpeted staircase. Upstairs, the interior of the restaurant is breathtakingly sumptuous with über-classy black and white velvet walls and huge arrangements of lush, exotic flowers at the front desk and in the middle of the restaurant. All the chair frames are made of some matt silver metal and the thickly padded seats and backs are covered in multicolored velour: orange, gold, red, green, blue, brown.

We're shown to what seems to be the best table in the place: an elevated platform next to a super-modern cascade fountain piece. Waiters swarm around our table pulling out chairs, bowing, scraping, smiling, nodding. Next to me, a waiter lifts the napkin from the charger plate, gently unfolds it, and courteously lays it across my lap. Bemused, I thank him. He nods solemnly in acknowledgment.

Another jacketed man flourishes menus at us. A complimentary, pink-tinged champagne cocktail appears magically on my right, but I notice that a glass of amber liquid is being offered to Dom. A young man of Middle Eastern descent smiles sweetly when I thank him.

A man oozing obsequiousness in a black suit materializes at Dom's elbow. The display of excessive servitude is quite frankly startling, but Dom seems accustomed to it.

'Would you like me to choose the wines to complement the dishes, Mr. Eden?' the man asks ingratiatingly. Ah, a sommelier. Well, well, I've never been to a restaurant that was swanky enough to hire a sommelier!

'Pair them with the lady's meal,' Dom says. 'And just my usual.'

'Very good, sir,' he says with a nod and a quick glance in my direction, and exits the scene.

I turn my attention to the menu. The combinations of ingredients are unusual and fascinating. I look up once and Dom is

watching me. For a moment we stare at each other then I feel myself start to color and have to drop my eyes back to the menu. When Dom lays his menu down I do the same. Almost instantly the headwaiter is at my side. We place our orders and he diplomatically compliments us on our excellent choices.

A small plate of beautifully colorful miniature amuse-bouches is placed in the middle of the table. The waiter who brought it explains what the little titbits are, but his French accent is so thick I catch only the words 'black radish', 'fromage frais' and 'steamed mussels with pickle and Guinness'. He disappears as silently as he had arrived.

I pick up one of the ceramic tasting spoons holding a little cube made from three brightly colored, unrecognizable ingredients, sitting in a pool of soy sauce, and slip it into my mouth. There's a delicate burst from the green base of avocado, the rich meaty taste of tuna tartare and a complete texture and taste change with the rice crispies and deep fried shallots on the top.

'Good?' Dom asks.

'Very,' I reply sincerely.

He pops one of the smoked salmon shells between his lips and suddenly I find myself hungrily watching his incredibly sexy mouth. I drag my gaze away quickly and cast it around the opulent room.

If his intention is to dazzle me then yes, I'm dazzled—the suit, the car, the impossible

 34

to miss deference of the waiting staff toward him, the splendor of the restaurant, the five star excellence of the food—but it doesn't mean a damn thing.

That strange look we shared in his empty restaurant is worth more to me than one thousand nights in the lap of unrivaled luxury. I know that moment is gone forever. The man in front of me is wearing a mask and he has no intention of ever letting me see underneath the mask again.

He is either with me now because he wants to take me to bed or he is trying to get some information out of me. Most likely a bit of both. I won't give him any information, but I also know I can't be the one to hurt him either. Not after what I saw this afternoon.

Tomorrow, I will tell Rob that I want to be taken off this case. He'll ask why, and I'll tell him that I don't feel comfortable around Mr. Dominic Eden. That is tomorrow. Tonight belongs to me and the man in the mask.

I take a sip of the delicious champagne cocktail and meet his gaze. 'I notice you don't have a Facebook page?'

FIVE

Ella

He stares at me. 'Is that a crime?'

'No,' I concede. 'But it is rather unusual.'

'Why?' he demands.

I shrug. 'Everybody uses some form of social media. Twitter, FB, MySpace, Picasa, Tsu, Instagram, Plaxo, Xing, Ning ... You can't be found on any platform.'

He bares his teeth suddenly in a pirate grin. And ooh ... devilishly attractive. My heart flutters a bit.

'Can it be,' he mocks softly, 'that HMRC's latest and most formidable weapon, the eighty million pound super-computer Connect, needs me to supply it with data so it can effectively spot signs of potential non-compliance from me?'

'Hardly,' I reply. 'Connect holds over a billion pieces of data collected from hundreds of sources. As it happens, a lack of

participation on social media is also "data". It indicates a desire to conceal suspicious activity.'

He raises one straight, raven-black eyebrow. 'Really?'

'Yes, *really*,' I say with emphasis.

At that precise moment, the sommelier appears with a bottle and tries to display the label to Dom, but Dom doesn't take his eyes off me. Not willing to be outdone, I stare back. When the bottle is uncorked, he makes a slight motion with his hand to indicate that he wants to dispense with the business of tasting the wine. The sommelier comes around to my side and fills my glass. When he goes around to Dom's glass, Dom gives a slight shake of his head. Quietly, the man slips the bottle back into the ice bucket and disappears.

I take a sip of wine. It is so smooth and ripe with different and distinct flavors that it makes every type of wine I have ever consumed seem like bootlegged versions of squashed grapes and vinegar.

'Just out of interest,' Dom says, 'what information does Connect hold about me?'

'And there I was thinking I was here to learn more about your business and not the other way around.'

'Touché.' He chuckles good-naturedly.

I smile faintly.

'So, what would you like to know about me?' he offers with a reckless smile.

I slip a steamed mussel into my mouth. It is so tender it melts on my tongue. I let it slide down my throat and wipe my lips on the napkin before I answer. 'I'd like to know why you aren't on social media.'

The broad shoulders lift, an almost Italian gesture. 'We're gypsies,' he says, as if that answers everything.

'And?' I prompt.

'By nature we distrust any form of surveillance, and as you've just confirmed, all forms of social media are Greeks bearing gifts.' A teasing quality slips into his voice. 'See, gypsies wouldn't have towed the Trojan horse into their city.'

'I don't want to be stereotypical or anything, but I honestly thought gypsies have always been rather brilliant horse thieves.'

His crystalline blue eyes twinkle with mischief. 'Ah yes. Perhaps it would have been a different matter if the horse had been real, or made of scrap metal. But being wooden ...'

I really want to laugh with him, but I suppress the urge. I'm *not* on a date. I cannot allow myself to like him. I'll just end up getting hurt.

We're interrupted by the arrival of our starters. My order of goat's cheese with roasted beet looks like a white and magenta millefeuille. I gaze at it with awe. Just as the amuse-bouches before, it is a precisely arranged work of art. Almost too beautiful to eat. Dom has seared scallops and walnuts served with a dinky pot of Parmesan brûlée

I cut into my millefeuille and fork a small piece into my mouth. It is so delicious I'm immediately struck by how much I'd love to be able to afford to bring my parents here, instead of all the cheap restaurants my tight budget forces me to take them to. I *know* they would never have tasted anything so refined and luscious, and it suddenly and painfully hits home that they probably never will. And just like that I no longer need to stop myself from liking him. That resentment for 'people like him' comes back into my gut. I welcome it like an old friend. It's better this way. I am too affected by him already.

'Why are you so afraid of surveillance if you're doing nothing wrong?' I ask.

'Why do you have curtains in your bedroom windows? Are you doing something wrong?' he shoots back.

'It's not the same thing,' I argue.

'Why isn't it? I don't want the government, its agents and a whole slew of marketers to have access to my private data. That's my business alone, and I take steps to keep it so. Why is that concept so foreign to you?'

'You'll be pleased to know that Connect holds very little information on you, or,' I continue, 'your brothers.'

He smiles a slow, satisfied smile.

Smile he should. Guarding his privacy has worked. He is a closed door to Connect's tentacles. All it managed to dig up was that at twenty-eight years old he has never made a

benefit claim. He doesn't own or co-own any property or business. Needless to say, I don't believe that for a second. Him not financially tied with anyone? As if! He has two bank accounts that show a pathetic amount of activity, mostly direct debits for utility bills. No overdraft. He has a credit card, but he won't even use it to pay for petrol. He hasn't flown with a commercial airline for as long as Connect has been running. One look at that tan tells me he didn't acquire it in London. Which only signifies he's leaving the country using other, private means.

I flash him a fake smile. 'It would appear that you've fooled the super-computer into believing that you're a rather uninteresting employee.'

He lifts his glass of whiskey. 'I don't know how you meant that to come out, but I have to say it kinda looks bad when you give the impression that you believe you're better than a super-computer.'

I smile through my irritation. 'Connect is an amazing invention. At the touch of a button it can show an incredibly detailed picture about a person that would have taken months of research before, but it has no intuitive powers. The department relies on investigators and analysts like me to validate the data and pick up unnatural patterns.'

'Unnatural patterns? Like what?' he asks, fishing for information.

Well, he's not getting anything but the obvious from me. 'Like *everything* I've seen

tonight. Like the clothes, the car, this restaurant.'

'So, you noticed my clothes,' he notes cheekily. It's hard to imagine that this is the same tormented man from this afternoon.

'One can hardly fail to notice that they're not off a department store's rack.' My voice is mild.

He widens his eyes innocently. 'I saved up for years to buy these clothes. The car belongs to the company, and I only come to this restaurant when I'm feeling particularly flush or on a really big date.'

'It's all a big joke to you, isn't it?' I accuse. I can feel myself losing my cool.

'It's not just a job for you, is it?' he asks curiously.

'No, it's not. It's a personal crusade.' I lean back as the waiting staff move in to efficiently and quickly clear away our plates. My wine is replenished and a fresh glass of whiskey is placed before Dom. I notice that he's not drinking any wine at all, which means that he ordered the bottle solely for me.

'So, you must hate people like me.'

'Hate might be too strong a word. Detest might be a bit closer.'

He looks at me with a perplexed expression as if he's trying to figure out a three-headed, ten-limbed, purple-striped creature. 'Why do you care so much what tax I pay? I couldn't give a rat's ass whether you pay yours or not.'

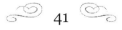

'Because people like you play the legal game and screw the country,' I accuse hotly.

'Trying to avoid paying more tax than you have to is not *screwing the country*. On the contrary, it's doing one's best to avoid being screwed by people like *you*. I'm paying the right amount of tax within the rules. Only a sanctimonious, pompous zealot would criticize someone for seeking every *legal* means possible to reduce their tax bill. Tax avoidance isn't wrong. It's perfectly sensible behavior.'

'Wow,' I gasp. 'This is a turn-up for the books. The tax dodger decides to take the moral high ground!'

He shrugs nonchalantly. 'Let not he who is houseless pull down the house of another, but let him labor diligently and build one for himself, thus by example assuring that his own shall be safe from violence when built—Abraham Lincoln.' He leans back, a smug smile on his face.

My main course—Dorset crab and black quinoa with tomato and Meyer lemon sauce—is put before me. It's a world-class visual treat, but I find I've completely lost my appetite.

'Bon appétit,' Dom says when we're alone again, and digs with relish into his Ahi tuna topped with caviar. It is lined with slices of zucchini that are so thinly sliced they're almost transparent.

I fold my arms over my chest. 'So, you think that you have a perfect right to pay

little or even no tax if possible, because you're wealthy enough to have access to devious accountants, slick lawyers, corrupt bankers and tax havens while the rest of us subsidize your operations by paying for the education and health care of your workforce, the roads you and your companies use, and the police deployed to guard your restaurants and nightclubs from trouble.'

He leans forward, his eyes glittering dangerously. 'If you truly feel that way then why don't you do something about the really big tax avoiders like Google, Starbucks, Microsoft and Apple?'

I sit up straighter in my chair. 'My mandate does not cover multinational companies.'

He raises one mocking eyebrow. 'Your mandate doesn't cover multinationals? How fucking convenient.'

'Another department deals with them,' I defend tensely.

He bursts into a sarcastic, cynical laugh.

I stare at him furiously. How dare he make out that I'm in some insidious way complicit in the wrongdoings of the multinational companies?

'Since you seem completely clueless, let me tell you how your department for policing the multinationals dealt with the big boys last year. Starbucks had sales of four hundred million pounds in the UK last year, but paid no corporation tax at all. It transferred some money to a Dutch sister company in a royalty

43

payment, bought coffee beans from Switzerland (hey! who knew Switzerland produces coffee beans, but there you go), and paid high interest rates to borrow from other parts of the business.' He pauses. 'Want to hear how they dealt with Amazon?'

I say nothing.

'I thought not. But here's the deal anyway. With sales in the UK of four-point-three billion last year, it reported a tax expense of just four-point-two million pounds. What percentage is that, Ella? Could that possibly be just nought-point-one percent?'

I know everything he's said is true, but I've always told myself that it's not my remit. If I do my job well then I've done my bit to make my country a better place. His arguments do not shake my foundations at all. I clamp my mouth shut and refuse to be drawn into an issue that has nothing to do with his tax situation—or me.

'Why so quiet, hmm? Is it because you already know that the same story is repeated with Google and Apple and every massive multinational? The obvious question that arises in any rational person's mind would be why should I not make my tax disappear too?'

I jut my jaw out aggressively. 'How about because it's morally wrong? Or because you care for the people of this country? Because your taxes will keep schools and hospitals from closing their doors? Because

you don't have to do something wrong just because others are doing it?'

He shakes his head. 'You know what you are, Ella?'

'You're obviously dying to tell me,' I say dryly.

'You're someone's attack dog. The question is whose? You've obviously been fooled into thinking you're the attack dog for the poor and oppressed, but answer this: Every year you collect more and more taxes, so, how is it then that every year there's less and less for public services?'

I scowl, but he's touched a raw nerve.

He sees my second of hesitation and presses his advantage. 'Did you know that since 2007 our government has committed to spending over a trillion pounds to bail out banks? What does it say about their priorities if they're able to find the money to save the banks, bomb Afghanistan, bomb Iraq, bomb Libya, and now they're wanting to start a fresh war in Syria, but cannot find the funds for schools and hospitals?'

I stare at him in dismay.

'The truth is there are billions to be gained by going after the big boys, but no one's doing it. On the day our government acts to squeeze these massive tax cheats you're welcome to break my balls about the morality of my tax avoidance schemes and lecture me about your utopian ideals of wealth redistribution. Until then, give me a fucking break.'

I pick up my glass of wine and drain it. I put it back on the table slowly. It's possible that without realizing it I've drunk far too much. My head feels foggy. In my incapacitated state, I'm unable to come up with a single suitable argument to support my cause. My heart knows that even though his argument seems logical, it's not right. It can't be.

He looks at me almost sadly. 'You remind me of that old Led Zepplin classic, *Stairway to Heaven*. You're the woman who believes that everything that glitters is gold and that you're buying a stairway to heaven. But your stairway is whispering in the wind, Ella.'

SIX

Ella

The strings of a lute are alone
Though they quiver with the same music.
—Khalil Gibran

Unable to meet his eyes, I stare blankly at a waiter refilling my glass. When he straightens the bottle I'm shocked to realize that I've drunk more than half of it. That on top of the vodka and the champagne cocktail! No wonder he's running rings around me with his flawed 'I'll pay if they pay' reasoning.

He moves closer. 'Are you drunk yet?' he whispers.

Up close and suddenly he seems wild and full of dirty promises. I lean toward him like a moth to a flame. 'Were you deliberately trying to get me drunk?'

'Wouldn't you if you were me?'

My mind chases its own tail. 'Why do you want me to be drunk?'

'Can you handle the truth?' His eyes are hooded.

'Of course.'

'Because you're the kind of inhibited woman who needs to be intoxicated before she can explore her deepest desires. This way, you don't have to be responsible for your actions. "I was so drunk," you can say to your best friend tomorrow morning.'

It's a far cry from the truth—I'd sleep with him without even a whiff of alcohol—but I'll be damned before I tell him that. 'Very confident of yourself, aren't you?'

'I like playing with fire, Miss Savage.'

His phone must have vibrated in his pocket because he takes it out and looks at it. 'Do you mind?' he asks.

I shake my head.

'Hey, Ma,' he says, and listens while she tells him something. 'She did?' he says, and smiles, and it is a genuine smile. A soft, warm smile. I stare at him in surprise. I don't want to know that he has a mother whom he obviously adores. And I realize I can't go through with my plan of sleeping with him for one crazy night. I know having sex with him will open a door and what comes through I might not be able to control. He has the capacity to hurt me. I am too affected by him. I feel things that I have never felt before.

His eyes lift up, meet mine, and the smile freezes. 'I've got to go, Ma, but I'll pass

48

by tomorrow. Give it to me then? OK. Bye.'
He puts his phone away.

I look him in the eye. 'I can't have sex with you.'

'Why not?' he asks huskily.

I lean back against the chair, the alcohol buzzing in my veins. There's a pulsing in my temples. Telling him the real truth is out of the question. The half-truth is the only option. 'Because you're a crook.'

His eyes flash with real fury. All that urbane and polite stuff before was just a façade. This is the real Dominic Eden. The hothead who can be exploited by the right person. Maybe even me.

'On what evidence are you basing your accusation?' he asks coldly.

'Instinct.'

'That won't hold up anywhere. Until you find some evidence to support your "instinct", I suggest you refrain from making such wild accusations.'

'I'll find it,' I say, knowing it is an empty threat. Tomorrow I walk away from him and this case forever. For now I'll pretend that I'm the big, tough tax investigator.

'I'm sure you'll try.'

'Don't underestimate me.' My voice actually sounds harsh.

He smiles: a megawatt smile. It takes my breath away, lights up the room and registers as another warning in my heated brain.

 49

I let my eyes travel down to his brown throat. It's not fair that a man should be this gorgeous. My eyes slide back upwards to those firm, kiss me slow lips, and up to his eyes. They are heavy-lidded. The eyelashes thick and stubby, the blue of his irises so intense they're piercing. To my horror, my alcohol-fueled body responds. My nipples tighten and harden.

'I need to go home,' I choke.

He lifts his hand. A waiter brings the check in a leather book. He opens it, glances at it, and leaves a wad of notes between the leather.

I play my part. 'Cash?' I taunt.

'Every fucking time.' His eyes suck me in.

I resist the pull. 'Why's that?'

'I like the smell of money.'

'People with things to hide pay with cash.'

'At the risk of repeating myself, people who don't want their bank and every fucking government surveillance agency in the world to have access to their entire fucking lives do, too. You ready to go?'

I nod and stand, swaying slightly.

His brows knit. It makes him all dark and brooding. Like my favorite hero of all time, Heathcliff. 'You all right?' he asks.

'Absolutely,' I say, and, straightening my shoulders, precede him out of the restaurant. We go back down the stairs. A man is coming up and he stares at me with

barefaced interest. As he passes us, Dom stops, puts his hands on either side of the man's head, and turns his face so that it's pointing straight ahead instead of at me. The man's eyes bulge with shock and fear. He's only a head shorter than Dom, but he looks like a scared rabbit in the jaws of a tiger.

I watch Dom pat the man's cheek condescendingly before he turns to me and we carry on down the stairs. I glance back and the man is walking on up, his head stiffly held forward, too frightened to turn around and look at either of us. Fuck! That was like a scene from a Mafia movie.

I turn toward Dom. 'What did you do that for?'

'Asshole was lucky. I was in a good mood. He was looking to get his head fucking kicked in.'

'Because?'

'Because he fucking looked at my woman, that's why.'

A totally inappropriate but powerful thrill flashes through me, lighting up cells that have never seen light in their sad little lives. For that second I want to be his woman, I want him to speak so possessively about me. But that second passes as fast as it made its unexpected visit, and an odd sense of loss replaces it. I never suspected that inside me was such a needy being. What the hell is the matter with me! I'm so mentally unhinged by my own pathetic reaction that

the words that leave my mouth are like cold, hard bullets.

'I'm not your woman.'

He glances at me, unembarrassed, unfazed, and without missing a beat says, 'He doesn't know that. I'd never disrespect another man by looking at the woman he's with like that.'

There's no more to be said after that.

She bends her head, and honey-blonde, silky hair tumbles over her shoulder. Something jerks inside me. Jesus, I can't do this. It's too fucking painful. She looks up at me, her eyes as large and enquiring as a child's.

'What's the matter?' she asks.

The look scorches me. 'Nothing.' My voice is harsh. I had not intended that.

She stiffens, her eyes becoming more distant.

I crack a smile and pretend to be the polite gentleman I've been all night long even though it kills me inside. I do it because I need her in my bed. I want to run my fingers along the wet seam of her pussy lips and I

want to see how fierce and wild she'll be when my cock plunges into her.

Maybe she can stop the pain.

When he opens the passenger door our hands accidentally touch and both of us draw back as if we've been burnt.

'Sorry,' I mumble.

He inhales sharply and says nothing.

I slide in and he closes the door for me. When he gets in I glance covertly at his long, strong body. It's as tense as a coiled spring. Then the car guns into action and we're speeding through the cool night air.

The car stops outside my little flat. I turn toward him. 'Thank you for dinner. I really—'

'I'll walk you to your door,' he says, cutting me short.

'I'll be fine,' I say, but he's already opened his door and slipped out of the car. I shut my mouth and stare straight ahead. I think I'm a bit petrified about what might happen next.

He opens the passenger door. I put my hand in his outstretched palm and, placing

my legs together, I swing them out as gracefully as I can and he heaves me out. He holds open the entrance door of my building and we walk together toward the lift. He presses the button to call it and it makes a clanking sound. It's stopped working again.

I turn to him. 'It's broke.'

'Thank God,' he mutters. 'I don't think I can bear the smell of piss at this time of night.'

I wave a hand in the air. 'Don't worry, you can go. I'll be fine. I always use the stairs, anyway.'

He looks down at me expressionlessly. 'I took the stairs when I came up to get you. I can't do bad smells. I only used the lift on the way down because of your high heels.'

'Oh!' I exclaim, blinking fast enough to have a seizure. 'All right, if you're sure,' I say airily, and, turning away from him, start walking toward the stairs.

We walk up three flights of stairs without saying much. Outside my door I bend my head and rummage around in my purse for my key. I fish it out and hold it up.

'Goodnight and thank—' I begin brightly and then I come to a dead stop.

He's staring at me in a way that should be outlawed. No man has *ever* looked at me like that. As if he's starving and I'm triple-seared rib-eye steak. I feel the breath rush out of me and I don't think I can remember how to take the next one. I'm still staring into his eyes with my mouth open when he takes the key out of my nerveless hand.

'This is a grave mistake,' I whisper.

'I need it, and you want it,' he says harshly.

He fits the key into the keyhole. I shake my head. 'It's wrong. We'll regret it.'

He opens the door and walks me backward through it. 'You might, I won't.'

He kicks the door shut. I take a deep breath and his eyes drop to my heaving chest.

'Dom,' I breathe.

He backs me up to wall, his mouth inches away from mine. His energy is like a force field that is pressing me to the wall. A soft growl rumbles in his throat. It's electrifying. My body responds by freezing. Blood rushes in my ears, deafening me, and every thought, sane or otherwise, flies out of my stunned brain. He cups the back of my head while his other hand comes around my waist like a band of steel and slams me into his hard body, crushing my breasts. It's a good thing he's holding me because my body feels boneless, as if I could melt and disappear into him.

I feel his breath waft over my face. It smells sweetish, like maraschino cherries soaked in alcohol. I've never felt so alive, or so vibrant, or so precious. I could have climbed mountains, flown to the stars, melted the sun. It's as if he's my secret dream. Something I've dreamed of and never known. I gasp with a mixture of shock and

desire, and he clamps his lips onto my open mouth.

It's like falling into a giant tidal wave.

And drowning. I don't see him produce the condom, tear the foil, or even feel him fit the rubber. It's all done while I'm sinking deeper and deeper. He snatches his mouth away. I gasp for air. Grabbing the edges of the slit in my red skirt, he rips it right up to the waist. My panties are flung, wet and torn, to the floor. His hands run down my back and over my ass, cupping and lifting me until I'm dangling off the ground at almost eye level with him. Slowly he grinds his erection against me.

Then he points his cock at my entrance and rams into me, hard. Enormous ... Foreign ... Dominating. The shock of the sheer size of him makes me grunt. My muscles convulse to accommodate the unexpected intrusion.

'Does this feel wrong?' he snarls.

I curl my legs around his thighs. 'Fuck you,' I spit, and squeeze his cock tight.

'Yesssss, do that. Just like that,' he approves hoarsely.

He withdraws and thrusts up into me, so forcefully that my body climbs the wall behind me.

'Argh,' I cry out, but in fact it feels fabulous. This is the way it was always meant to be.

'Want it harder?' he asks, his voice raspy.

'Yeah,' I whimper.

He slams into me again and I start to quake: Oh fuck! I'm ready to come apart—right here—right now. Electric volts shoot through my system. My body begins to tense and contract. My heart pounds so loudly I hear it from the edges of consciousness. I try to push against it, but I'm standing in the way of a juggernaut. I climax with my head thrown back and screaming. He carries on thrusting through my orgasm until with a roar he, too, climaxes. I'm still panting hard when his eyes meet mine.

We stare at each other. Enemies again.

He pulls out of me and I feel a pang. Loss. Having him inside me felt right. Without him inside me I can think rationally again, and I'm suddenly ashamed and angry with myself. What an idiot I am.

He allows me to slide down his body, but when I try to wriggle away, his grip is steely. I quickly push the flaps of my skirt down over my throbbing sex and trembling thighs.

'Don't be expecting a repeat of that,' I say through gritted teeth.

He loses the condom, zips up, and fixes his eyes on me. His voice is unyielding. 'Don't kid yourself, baby girl. I'll have a repeat whenever I please.'

'Don't bet on it,' I snap.

'I'll bet my last tax dollar on it,' he says. He takes my chin in his hand. It's a hard man's hand, the fingers long and square. He

pulls my face up and gazes down at me, his eyes deliberately veiled. I stare up at him resentfully.

'I'll pick you up at seven tomorrow night,' he says with a frown.

'I have another appointment,' I lie.

Something dangerous flashes in his eyes. 'Cancel it,' he says brutally.

I open my mouth to argue, but he catches the hair at the back of my neck in his fist and covers my mouth with his palm. I stare up at him with wide, half-fearful, half-excited eyes.

'I haven't even scratched the surface of what I fucking want to do to you,' he growls.

Then he's gone, shutting the door quietly behind him.

My chest heaves as if I've just run a marathon.

'It's just a physical thing. Just sex,' I whisper to the empty air.

I, stalker

I stand on the street and stare up at her bedroom window. For a long time I don't see anything. Then ... her shadow passes ... fleetingly. I behold the momentary vision

eagerly. She is wearing something diaphanous and white, and her hair swims down her back and catches the light in such a way that each silky lock seems to be individually illuminated. It gives her a wild look, as if her very soul is untamed and free. She moves away.

I wait another hour, but she never again appears at the window. I stare up at the window even after the light goes out. What a thrill it used to be to watch her while she was unaware. I spent hours imagining her in bed, her beautiful hair spread across her pillow, wondering which duvet set she was using that day. But today there is no joy at all even in the mind fuck of imagining her masturbating, climaxing, and falling asleep with her thighs wide open, her pussy wet and ready for me.

Hatred bursts into my gut like burning lava. Even though he had stayed for a short time I know he fucked her. He had the air of man who had shot his load. Proud, satisfied, disheveled.

I never thought she would betray me in this way. I feel like rushing up to her apartment. What a fucking shock she'd get. My feet start to move and then I catch myself.

Patience. Patience.
She will be mine...

SEVEN

Ella

I knock on Rob's door.

'Come in,' he calls.

I enter. 'You wanted to see me?'

He beckons me over to his desk with his finger. 'Have you made another appointment with the wanker's accountant?'

I know exactly to whom he's referring, but I feign ignorance. 'Which wanker?'

He looks at me with unconcealed irritation. 'How many wankers are we dealing with? That Eden wanker, obviously.'

'Er ... not yet. I didn't know when you would be coming back to work. How are you today?'

'Fine,' he dismisses curtly. 'Check my diary and make another appointment as soon as possible.'

I shift my weight from one foot to the other with the realization that apparently Dominic Eden is personal for both Rob and me. Me because I crossed the line last night and probably will again tonight, and Rob because Dom snubbed him by refusing to shake his hand, so he's decided to show him who the real 'boss' in this scenario is. Before yesterday he was just doing his job. Today he's out for blood.

Unfortunately this puts an end to my plans to exit gracefully. A) In this frame of mind, Rob wouldn't 'get' my reason. And B) I can't walk away and allow Rob to misuse his power and destroy Dom. I've seen him in this mode before, when people rub him up the wrong way, and I know just how vindictive he can be. Once he gets like this, he always demands the maximum penalties. Prison, if possible.

I close the door and walk into his room. 'Sir, do you ever wonder if what we're doing is right?'

His eyes fly up to meet mine. 'No.' He pauses and leans back in his chair. 'What's up with you, Savage?'

My face flames. God! If he knew what I did yesterday.

'Nothing,' I reply, keeping my tone light and easy. 'I was just wondering how it is that we always go after the middle and upper middle classes. We never seem to target the truly big corporations and the truly rich one percent who should be paying billions in taxes but don't.'

He looks at me as if I'm stupid. 'Because that's not our job. Our mandate is to go after

the middle and upper middle classes. Going after the big boys is somebody else's job.'

'Whose job is it?'

'How would I know?' he says with a shake of his head.

'From what I can see, nobody's going after them.'

'Are you surprised?'

'What do you mean?'

He sighs. 'The best description of taxation I've ever heard was from one of our ex-Prime Ministers, Denis Healey. He, very sensibly, compared it to plucking a live goose: the aim is to extract the maximum number of feathers with the minimum amount of hissing. Plucking the corporations would create the kind of hissing we're unprepared to handle. They have the best lawyers and the most talented accountants who'd run rings around us. We're never going to get anything out of them. It would just be a pointless exercise.'

'So we go after the small and medium-sized fish because we can't catch the big white sharks and the killer whales?'

'Got it in one.'

'But that's so wrong.'

'No, it's not. Every year we recover billions from these slimy bastards.'

'And do what with that money?'

He looks at me with a sneer. 'Our shakedown pays for schools, hospitals, roads, people to collect your rubbish, police, fire services. Need I go on?'

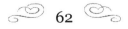

'But it's still unfair,' I say softly.

He leans forward and steeples his fingers. 'Life *is* unfair, Savage. Is it fair that one child is born the great-grandson of the Queen of England with a golden spoon in his mouth, and another child, through no fault of its own, is born to starve in Africa?' He pauses to look at me with an expectant expression. When I say nothing, he adds, 'Now, go make that appointment with the wanker's accountant, will you? That's one goose I want to see plucked and cooked until crisp.'

I bite my lip. 'I don't know about his account, Rob. The computer flagged the tax return because there was one incorrect figure, but you and I know it's probably just a simple accounting error. If that one figure is adjusted as his accountant proposes there's no reason at all to suspect there's any tax fraud going on.'

His eyes narrow. A mean look comes into them. 'What's the matter with you today, Savage? Have you gone soft in the head?'

I take an involuntary step back. There's something cruel about Rob. I'd hate to be on the receiving end of his fury.

He goes on coldly. 'It's as obvious as the nose on my face that this restaurant is not paying the correct amount of tax. They never are. Dig hard enough and there's always something to be found. At the very least I expect to extract a massive penalty and interest for our time and effort.'

'Right. I'll go and make that appointment now,' I say, and quickly exit his office before he deduces more than he already has about my stance on the matter.

I go back to my desk and lean my forehead against my palm. What a bloody mess. Nigel Broadstreet has already called twice to speak to me and left his mobile number. I dial it and he answers the call.

'Mr. Broadstreet? Ella Savage, HMRC, here.'

'Good morning, Miss Savage.'

'Yes, I'm calling to reschedule our appointment.'

'Yes, of course. When would be convenient for you?'

I look at the computer screen showing both Rob's diary and mine. 'How about Monday, ten a.m.?'

'Excellent. Same place?'

'That will be fine.'

'I'll see you there, then.'

'Um ... Will Mr. Eden be attending, too?'

He pauses as if surprised. 'No,' he says very firmly. 'Mr. Eden is an employee who has very little information about the accounting side of things. As I explained before, and will prove during our appointment, this whole situation is an error made by a trainee, which can be rectified quite easily.'

'Fine. I'll see you Monday. Please don't be late.'

He coughs uncomfortably. 'Of course.'

'Goodbye, Mr. Broadstreet.'

'Goodbye, Miss Savage.'

I end the call and schedule the appointment into our diaries. Afterwards, I call my mother and confirm that I'll be picking her and my father up at twelve. Then I call down to John to remind him that I'll need to borrow the 'official business' car at eleven thirty. I lean back in my chair. Dom will not be at the meeting. Thank God. I honestly don't think I could act normal if he was there watching me with those eyes, knowing he's been inside me.

As planned, I pick my parents up at twelve and we have lunch at a local pub. The food tastes like what it costs—£5.99 for two courses and £9.99 for three—but my father seems to be glad of the change of scenery, and my mother's in a good mood. So, it's a nice, easy lunch.

After that, we all troop back into the car and I drive to Tesco to do the weekly big shop for my parents. Because I felt bad yesterday that I could never take them to a place like the Rubik's Cube, I start picking up stuff that's more expensive than I'd normally choose and place it in the trolley.

My mother touches my arm. She looks worried. 'That's too expensive for us, darling. Just the economy version will do,' she says.

'No,' I say with sadness in my heart. 'I want to treat you and Dad to something better than economy this week.'

'But, darling,' my mother whispers, 'you'll leave yourself short.'

I smile at her. 'It's only this one week, Mum. Next week we'll go back to the economy stuff, OK?'

I fill the trolley with fine ham, expensive cheeses, two good cuts of sirloin, some of Tesco's finest desserts, a lovely boxed Tesco's Finest carrot cake, all butter croissants, branded ice cream, two duck breasts and organic walnut bread. The bill, when it's rung up, is shocking. It's almost double what I usually spend shopping for economy stuff. My mother gives me a 'let's put it all back' look, but, ignoring her, I slide my credit card into the reader and key in my PIN.

I return to work at two p.m. to find a large brown box inside an Argos plastic bag. For one second I think my mother has sent me a gift. She does buy stuff from there, but then why would it arrive on my desk when I've just returned from spending time with her?

I walk toward the bag with a frown on my face. I take the brown box out of the bag and open it. Inside, there's another box, only this box is from an expensive boutique. I

quickly drop it back into the brown box and put everything back into the Argos bag. My face feels hot and my heart is beating fast in my chest.

Now I know exactly who the package is from. I stuff the bag under my table, switch on my computer, and stare blankly at the screen. It occurs to me that whoever he got to send the box to me went to a lot of trouble to make it seem as if I was just receiving some cheap thing from Argos. For that I'm grateful. The last thing I need is my work colleagues thinking I'm being bribed by tax evaders.

Lena, from down the hall, puts her head around my door. 'You got your package then?'

'Um ... yeah.'

She comes in. 'So what's in it?' she asks nosily.

'Oh, just my mother sending me something for the flat. Probably crockery.'

'Oh.' She scrunches up her face as if to say, 'Nothing interesting, then.'

I shrug as if replying, 'That's life, what can you do?'

She brightens. 'Do you want to come with us for a drink tonight?'

'Uh ... No. Not tonight. I'm a bit tired.'

'Oh, come on. It's Friday.'

'I know, but I'm too tired.'

'You sure?'

'Yeah. You have fun, though.'

The first thing I do when I get home is open the brown box and take out the expensive box. There's an envelope attached to it. I pull it off and extract the card.

To replace the one I ruined.
Dom

His handwriting is bold and not the prettiest, but like him it oozes power and confidence. I open the box. Tucked amid white tissue paper is something red. I take it out and gasp. Wow!

It's the most beautiful dress I've ever seen. It has a slit at the back and even looks like it's my size. In a daze I run my fingers over the soft material. I've never owned anything so fine in my life.

Carefully, I hang the dress on a hanger and hook it on the door handle of my closet. Then, lying on the bed, I open the box of handmade chocolates, and, while eating them, admire the dress. The chocolates are delicious. The dress is fabulous. But I don't like how confused I am about things I used to be so sure of.

In one hour Dom will be here.

EIGHT

Dom

I step up to the shower, turn it on, and the jet of hot water cascades down my body, relaxing my tightly wound muscles. I close my eyes and she fills my thoughts like an exotic perfume. Her eyes, blue and Bratz-doll enormous, flash into my mind. All day I've been haunted by their damn beauty. I know I'm being reckless, but I don't care.

I'm gonna have her and fuck the consequences.

So many women have lain in my bed. They come, they go. They taste like fucking dry bread and tap water. A man needs to eat, so I filled my belly, but all the time I wanted honey and sweet flesh. A body that begs me to take it even when its owner doesn't want me to.

Ella.

Ella of the zebra shoes, sexy calves and the perfect ass. Oh, that ass! What I could do

with such an ass. So, yeah, I'm gonna fucking risk it again today, just for that adrenalin rush of opening her thighs and ramming my dick straight into her wet, tight pussy while she sucks my tongue.

My mind replays the moment I threw her against the wall and fucked her as her mouth hung slack and a rush that I'd forgotten I could feel pulsed into my cock, engorging it, making it ache. I clutch it in my hand and it hums ... for her creamy body.

Soon, my friend. Soon.

I close my eyes and clear my head. Sometimes it feels as if I'm plunging off a cliff into the deep blue ocean. Maybe there are rocks under the surface. Maybe I won't survive. Maybe she won't take away the pain. Maybe she'll stand on the cliff edge and watch me bleed to death instead, but so be it. I can't stay away from her, even if it means my own destruction. I must see her soft hands lift her dress up and willingly offer me *everything.*

I must taste her honey again.

Ella

I keep my bedroom windows open, and when I hear the distinctive growl of the Maserati's V8 engine I lean out of the window and call down to him as soon as he cuts the noise. He looks up, surprised, and as darkly beautiful as an avenging angel.

'Don't come up, there's a parking attendant up the road. I'll come down,' I holler down to him.

'Well, hurry up then,' he shouts up.

I take one last look at myself in my pretty yellow sundress before running out of my flat and skipping down the three flights of stairs. As I step out into the street I see that Dom has come out of his car and is leaning his butt against it. My heart does a little dance. He looks super-edible in a black T-shirt, blue jeans and pristine Timberland boots. His arms are crossed, and my eyes greedily rove over the thick muscle cords. His eyes are as bright as gems and are focused on me. Hit by an unnatural attack of shyness (What? Me, shy?) I pause uncertainly by the entrance door.

'Hey, sexy,' he drawls.

'There's a parking attendant walking toward us with a very determined expression on his face,' I say as nonchalantly as I can.

He replies by opening the passenger door with a flourish. I walk toward him with a smile.

He grabs my arm. 'You're one incredibly beautiful woman, you know,' he says.

The compliment goes straight to my head and makes my skin burn. I have to pretend to look down at my shoes to hide my flustered face. He lets go of my arm and I slip into the seat. I turn my head to watch his fine ass go around the back of the car. He gets into the driver's seat and closes the door.

'Thanks for the dress. It's beautiful,' I say quickly, 'but I can't accept it. It's too expensive.'

He frowns down at me. 'It's just a replacement. I ripped your skirt yesterday.'

'Well, it's too expensive.'

'Well, I was *very* sorry,' he says with a glint in his eyes.

'It could be deemed a bribe.'

'Let me tell you how tonight and every night that we spend together is going to go down. We are never discussing my tax situation, or my finances, or any of that shit we talked about last night. You want that kind of information, you'll have to talk to Nigel. We are just going to eat, talk, fuck and have fun.'

'Rob and I have an appointment to see your accountant next week,' I inform him

quickly. 'I'm saying this up front so there's no misunderstanding about the investigation. We are going ahead with it.'

'Good,' he says casually.

'You don't sound worried.'

'That's probably because I'm not.'

I look at him curiously. 'Why not? Most people in your shoes would be.'

'Why should I be? I haven't done anything wrong, and Nigel will finally get to do what he's paid a shitload to do.'

'Look, we won't ever talk about your tax situation again, but I have to warn you that you really pissed Rob off the other day when you refused to shake his hand. He took it as a personal insult, and I think he's going for maximum damage.'

A soft look comes into his eyes. 'Thank you for the warning. It means something to me.' Then he grins. 'But it's totally unnecessary. I meant to piss that asshole off. He's like a little bully on a power trip. In school he would have been one of those boys who joined a gang to terrorize all those smaller and weaker than them.'

It's startling how you can spend weeks and months with someone and be totally blind to their true personality. In one sentence Dom has described Rob's entire MO. Something I'd shut my mind to because I truly believed we were doing it for the greater good. But now I'm not so sure anymore.

Are Rob and I bullies? We threaten ordinary, hardworking people who've salted away something for their old age, so they don't have to depend on their children to buy them the necessaries the way my poor parents do, with prison sentences and force them to pay up. When possible, we even go into their bank accounts and help ourselves to their hard-earned money. We do it all because we can. And yet the multinationals, the super rich, the old money families who already have everything tied up in untouchable trust funds, we allow to get away with paying laughable amounts of tax or no tax at all.

Yeah. I guess the hard truth is, we are shameless bullies.

The idea disturbs me greatly, but I don't share my thoughts with Dom. Instead, I shrug slightly and say, 'Just ask Nigel to be careful. Rob can be really vindictive.'

'You know those hotshot accountants the multinationals use?'

My ears prick up. 'Yeah ...'

'We stole Nigel from them. Let Rob pit himself against Nigel. It'll be interesting to see if my accountant is actually worth his huge salary.'

I don't get to answer him because the parking attendant is standing outside the car next to me. To my surprise, he doesn't berate Dom the way he does other drivers with lesser cars. Instead, he asks in a totally awed voice, 'How fast can this beauty go?'

'I never took her over a hundred and fifty mph,' Dom says.

The man shakes his head admiringly and lets his eyes caress the smooth lines of the car. 'She's a beauty, man. I'd exchange my wife for a car like this.'

Dom laughs, kisses the pad of his thumb, and guns the car. The attendant watches us take off with a wistful expression.

'Where are we going?' I scream over the noise.

'My place,' he says.

We park in an underground car park beneath a posh building in Chelsea and get into a lift smelling of disinfectant. Both of us face the gleaming doors as we're silently and quickly whisked up to the top floor. His apartment is one of two on the top floor. As soon as he opens the front door, I say, 'Wow!' Most of the walls are made of glass and the view is breathtaking.

'Oh my God! You can see across the river for miles out.'

He chucks his keys onto a metal container shaped like a leaf on the sideboard while I look around in amazement. The way homes in designer magazines look. Spotless, not a scratch or mark anywhere, fabulous furniture, everything color-coordinated with

one or two bold splashes here and there, the floors shining with polish, and a bowl of fruit on a statement coffee table.

'Does anyone actually live here?'

He looks at me strangely. 'I live here.'

'Wow, then you must have a shit-hot cleaner.'

'I'll tell Maria you said that,' he says with a grin.

I grin back foolishly.

'Come on. I'll show you the balcony,' he says and we cross the vast open-plan space. Our footsteps echo in the ultra-modern emptiness of the place. He opens the tall glass doors and I step outside.

'This is amazing,' I exclaim looking at the city bathed in the glow of the evening sun.

'Yeah, it is, isn't it? When you live somewhere for some time you start forgetting how beautiful you once thought it was.'

'You're very lucky,' I say sincerely.

His face closes over. 'It's still too early to say,' he says cryptically.

'No, you're already luckier than all the children who live in rubbish dumps in the Philippines and all the slave workers in China and India and all the homeless people in London.'

He looks down at me, and for a long time he doesn't say anything. Then he raises his finger and pushes away a skein of hair that the wind has undone from my face. His fingers feel hard and warm against my skin. I

have to resist the impulse to rub my face against his hand like some needy puppy. Thank God, he takes his hand away before I do something I'll forever regret.

'Sometimes you can be happier on a rubbish dump than in a palace,' he says.

'Do you really believe that?'

'I don't believe it, I know it. Growing up my family was dirt poor and yet we were happy. Fiercely happy.'

I stare up at him. In the sunlight his eyes are like blue crystals with silver flares, the pupils seeming too large for a man.

'People don't understand what wealth does. Wealth makes you more dissatisfied. You buy a house, you fill it with the best, then you buy another, you fill that with the best; you buy a yacht, then a plane; you buy a vineyard and then you buy a bigger yacht, and a bigger plane. Then you start a luxury car collection. And you never ever come to a place where you think, "That's enough now. Why earn any more? I couldn't spend it all in my lifetime even if I tried. I'll just stop working and relax, enjoy all I have." No, you just keep on pushing yourself, constantly expanding the business. It's why billionaires in their eighties put in eighteen hour days.'

I think of my parents. They're poor, yes, but they're happy in their small world outside the rat race. And except for my resentment of the people who don't pay their taxes, I love my little matchbox flat and my little life.

'Are you hungry?' he asks suddenly, jerking me away from my thoughts.

'Ravenous,' I admit.

And he laughs. 'Good. There's plenty of food.'

I hear his laugh inside my chest. 'What're we having? A takeaway?'

'Sort of.'

His idea of a sort of takeaway and mine are worlds apart. Mine is a small pepperoni pizza with garlic bread, or chicken biryani and poppadoms, or a quarter crispy duck and special fried noodles from one of the takeaway joints inside the five-mile free delivery radius. His is a three-course meal from one of his restaurants.

The food—well, the raw ingredients—is brought by a man in a chef's uniform whom Dom introduces as Franco. Franco then proceeds to cook and serve us as we sit at the dining table. I take a careful sip from my glass of wine. I woke up with a massive hangover this morning and I don't want to repeat the experience tomorrow.

'So, you can't cook,' I say, cutting into my perfectly baked leg of milk-fed lamb.

'Nope.' Holding his food at the side of his mouth, he says, 'My brother Shane can, though.'

'He's the youngest, isn't he?'

'No, my sister Layla is. He's the second youngest.'

I pick up a dab of artichoke and pearl barley mash at the end of my knife. 'Ah, yes. I

 78

forgot. He's the youngest boy. Being a stay-at-home mother, your sister didn't quite make it on to our radar. But she's married to a rather ... um ... interesting character, isn't she?'

He leans back and looks at me expressionlessly. 'He may be a rather ... um ... interesting character, but outside of my brothers I'd rather have BJ guard my back than I would any other man on earth. He's a totally straight and loyal guy. Maybe one day you'll meet him.' He smiles. 'He might not like you too much, though. As you've probably figured out, us gypsies have no love for tax collectors.'

'And yet here I am.'

He takes a sip of his whiskey and puts it down on the table, then remarks almost to himself, 'Yes, yet here you are. Real enough to touch.'

Whatever the thought was that passed through his head, it made him suddenly pensive.

'Why are you doing this?' I blurt out.

He looks up at me, one sooty eyebrow raised. 'Doing what?'

'Fraternizing with the hated tax collector.'

He gives my question serious consideration and then says the most unexpected thing. 'It is a lucky man who finds an enemy who is so intoxicating.'

I frown. Hearing him say that is surprisingly wounding. 'We're not enemies,' I say softly.

His eyes narrow until they are dark slits. 'Ah, but we are, sweet Ella. We just find each other physically irresistible. That is all. *Never* make the mistake of thinking otherwise.'

NINE

Ella

We're having sweet grapes and cheese from Hervé Mons on the balcony when Franco comes out to say that he's leaving.

'Thank you for a really delicious meal. I'd never tasted Sauternes jelly until tonight,' I say with a smile.

He bows. 'I'm glad. Maybe I will cook for you again,' he says, and then shoots a wary look at Dom.

'I'll look forward to that,' I say.

'Ciao, bella.'

'Ciao, Franco,' I say, surprised at how normal my voice sounds. Quite frankly, I'm more than a little tipsy. From the moment Dom made that statement about us being enemies who find each other sexually irresistible, everything changed for me. Until then, I'd allowed myself to fall into a ridiculous fantasy that I was dating the most gorgeous man on earth. I was actually drifting through my evening in a cloud of naive happiness, dreaming of a life together with him. A slice of heaven with two kids and a demented puppy. How stupid. As if someone like him would end up with someone like me.

I think I might even know the exact moment I got caught up in the fairy tale. When I was lying in bed looking at the red dress he sent me. It was so special, and I've never been given anything so splendid by anyone—ever. In fact, no one I know can even afford to buy such expensive items. I guess I got totally sucked into my outlandish piece of fiction when I tried on the dress and it fit me like a dream.

But really, who can blame me? It was such a delicious fantasy.

When I was a girl, I always, always wanted to be Cinderella. I wanted to go to the ball all dressed up in a glittery blue gown and have a handsome prince fall in love with me. At midnight I'd drop my glass slipper and my prince would come looking for me. He would search high and low, and no one else would do. The slipper was mine. The man was mine. Dom is the prince I've always dreamed of, and subconsciously I was acting out my childhood dream.

It was the throbbing emptiness inside me that made me forget my good decision to drink carefully, and I became stupidly reckless. I think I've consumed more than half a bottle of wine on my own. Again. Dom

never comments, just watches, and silently refills my glass. He doesn't even seem to care that I've gone strange and our conversation has become stilted. The harsh comment was designed to keep me at a distance. I guess he didn't want to lead me up the garden path. He wanted me to have no illusions. We're having sex and we're having fun.

Yay! What fun.

Dom uncurls his long frame and walks Franco to the door. Their voices roll through me as they cross the apartment. Feeling restless, I stand up. Whoa. Why is the floor moving? I put a foot in front of me, and another, and another, and I'm leaning on the railing. The city glitters like a bed of lights below. I hear the front door close and then Dom is back on the balcony. I turn around slowly. A wind has risen and it whips my hair into my eyes. I use both my hands to hold it in place.

He doesn't come closer. He just stands there watching me. I can't see his expression because the light is behind him, but his body is tense and taut. I think of how he pounced on me yesterday. I think of how shamelessly I responded.

'I think I'd like another drink,' I slur to him.

'Sure. What d'you want?' His voice is cool and distant. He really doesn't give a shit about me.

'I'll have that thing I saw Franco swigging from the freezer.'

 83

I can't be sure, but I think he smiles. 'OK. Do you want to come in? It's getting a bit cold.'

'So, what do you care?'

He walks up to me and threads his fingers through mine. 'To be honest, you look like you're about to fall over the railing, and I'd feel a lot better if we went in.'

'Yeah?'

He sighs. 'Christ, you're so drunk.'

'I thought you liked me drunk.'

'Come on. Let's get you some grappa.'

We go into his kitchen and I sit on the counter while he opens the freezer.

'Is that ice cream I see in there?' I ask interestedly.

He pulls the carton out.

'Let me see that. Gin and tonic ice cream! Where on earth did you get this from?' I exclaim enthusiastically.

'My sister buys it. She loves the stuff, but she's on this strict organic diet, so she keeps a tub here so the only time she can have it is when she's here. But I believe there might be a tub at Shane's, Jake's, and my mum's, too.' His face softens while he's talking about his sister, and suddenly I feel sad. I want this beautiful, beautiful man for myself, but he doesn't want me. Yeah, he wants me to have sex with, but not all of me in sickness and in health, till death do us part.

He looks at me with amusement. 'Would you rather have the ice cream instead of the grappa?'

I have to think this one out. 'Can I have the grappa poured over the ice cream?' I ask.

He makes a face. 'Seriously?'

'Seriously,' I insist.

I pop myself on a high chrome stool—and, believe me, that's some feat when you're feeling the way I am—and I put my elbows on the gleaming surface of the island and watch him scoop the ice cream out. Gosh, the way he scoops ice cream is so yummy, I want to pour the melted stuff down his body and lick it off him. He picks up the bottle of grappa and looks at me.

'You sure about this?'

I wave my hand to indicate that he should continue with the task of pouring.

He pours the ice-cold grappa over the ice cream and places it in front of me. He opens a drawer, finds a spoon and lays it beside the bowl. Actually, it looks quite delicious. I might have found a winning combination here.

I take the spoon, dig it into the concoction and put it into my mouth. Ooooh! My eyes widen and my mouth starts moving sideways. Oh!

His reaction is admirable. He shoves the bowl under my chin just as I spit it out.

'Sorry,' I apologize.

'It was a vile combination,' he concedes, handing me a paper towel.

I wipe my mouth and tongue. 'Oh dear, that was not very sexy, was it?' I say weakly. How was I to know that gin and tonic ice cream with grappa poured over it would be so evil?

'Actually,' he says, his irises growing, 'everything you do is sexy, sweet Ella. Can't you tell? I've been wanting to fuck you for hours.' He tilts his head. 'My bedroom is that way.' Slowly, I turn my head in the direction he's indicated.

'Get naked and sit on the edge of the bed,' he commands.

TEN

Dom

Her eyes flash with surprise, but she obeys me without a word. Desire is like the burning heat of a midday Sicilian sun on my skin as I watch her take swaying steps toward my bed. She stops at the bedroom door and looks around the room. A sigh escapes her. It is the wistful sigh of poor people the world over. Even though I have only stood at her front door and scanned the interior of her home, I know that my bedroom is bigger than her entire flat.

If she weren't so proud, I'd take her for my mistress. Set her up in a swanky apartment and shower her with gifts. Then I'd never have to feel guilty about using her.

She goes into the dimly lit room and I wait a few minutes. I have something to do before I follow her. I walk up to the doorway to my bedroom and halt.

The bright light coming in from behind me falls on her naked body. There are two kinds of women: the very slim woman who looks better in clothes, and her more rounded counterpart who looks better, much better, naked. She is the latter.

She's a waking dream.

Just like those great beauties that my granddad used to perve over. Even their names evoke a lost time—Brigitte Bardot, Marilyn Monroe, Raquel Welch.

Ella Savage is curvy and creamy white. Her breasts are not the perfect silicone planets I'm used to, but they are deliciously full and round. The areolae are sweet pink, barely darker than her skin, upon which her nipples protrude like swollen buds. My gaze moves down to the wasp-waist and the gorgeously rounded hips. Her pubic bush, the same dark blonde as her hair, is neatly trimmed.

I take a deep breath. The moment is surreal with silence and anticipation. It is as if I'm not part of it, but watching it happen on a movie screen.

'Lean back and rest your weight on your hands,' I order. Even to my ears my voice sounds harsh. Strange, because I don't feel harsh at all. Inside, I'm melting like a marshmallow over a flame.

I watch her arch her body back sensuously, her chest pushing out and up. Even so, she's not flaunting it. She simply sits there and allows me to look at her.

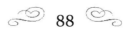 88

'Open your legs.'

I watch her spread them, but it's only a shy-open. There's more to go. A lot more. Between the intriguing paleness of her thighs, full, luscious lips beg for a tongue to part them open. Taste them. Suck them. Fuck them. The desire to crawl up to her and eat her out fills me.

'Put your feet up on the bed.'

Another woman would have scooted up the bed for more space, but she doesn't. She simply obeys the command exactly as it has been given. Her breathing increases as she moves to obey. A graceless, almost vulgar movement, but I actually like that, it's more real. She plants both her feet on the bed so her knees press up against her breasts.

I walk toward the liquid dripping from her pink seam like a man in a trance. I grab her hips and swipe my tongue along the swollen, succulent flesh. My body shudders. I was right. *Honey.* She's pure honey. She throws her head back and moans. With that un-doctored sound of ecstasy, the whole world ceases to exist for me. There is only my tongue and her sweet pussy.

'I want you to watch me eat you,' I tell her.

She brings her head forward and we stare at each other in wonder while I eat her until she comes rocking, arching, shrieking, and squirting shamelessly into my mouth.

Ella

My breath hasn't even returned to normal and already his dark shape is hovering above me, his palm gliding over my nipples, fingers trailing on my collarbone. All my senses heighten and my sex aches for his touch. In the shadows that envelop us I can hear his heart pounding hard. Only one side of his face is illuminated, and it is an expression of fierce concentration, as though I'm something so exquisitely fragile that the least wrong move could break me. He raises his eyes and meets mine. His are gleaming pools of *hunger*.

His mouth swoops down and covers a nipple. It's hot and rough, as if he's trying to brand me with his mouth. Shock flares in my veins.

'Oh!' I gasp, my whole body trembling with sexual intoxication.

Watching me intently he takes the nipple between his teeth and pulls. I whimper. But the glimmer of momentary pain is a tease from a master seducer. He starts sucking the way you would if you wanted to give someone a hickey. The sensation is electrifying.

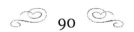

It feels as if my intoxicated mind is playing tricks on me. There is no doubt about the expertise of his technique. A burning desire rises within me as every muscle in my body stretches and tightens. I clench my hands helplessly. The hot mouth leaves as his other hand arrives between my legs.

'Open up,' he purrs. His breath is sweet as it dances between our lips.

I splay my legs open and he pushes a long finger into me.

'More,' I moan.

'Patience, Ella,' he whispers and withdraws even that finger.

I look up at him with begging eyes. He cannot know how much I want him, but I'm past caring. I want to stay forever in this world where there's no one else but us. He slides his hands under my ass cheeks and smiles. There's something mysterious and wild in that smile. I fix my eyes shut.

'Look at me,' he instructs.

I snap them open and watch completely spellbound as his mouth draws closer and closer.

Oh, my sweet baby Jesus! Another! In which dimension does a woman get two face cakes in one go?

His hot, velvety tongue laps at the warm juice dripping from my pussy. He drinks it as if it is the finest nectar. Lost in the exhilarating pull of his technique, I look deep into his eyes as shudders ripple through my body. He plunges his tongue deep into me

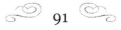

and I shake violently. His tongue, a muscular, practised thing, goes for the kill. His mouth encircles my swollen clit while it sucks!

Fuck! How it sucks. Why do Americans say it sucks when bad times hit them? It's fucking great when it sucks.

His fingers slip inside. Two, or is it three? Rough as his kisses had been. I'm too lost in the throes of a building orgasm to know or care.

'I'm coming,' I shout.

'Not yet,' he growls, but there's no way I can hold it any longer.

My thighs are already trembling uncontrollably. Every inch of me is tingling. I try to slither away, but it's too late. I prepared myself, but I could NEVER have imagined the explosion that the second eat-out brings.

It is indescribably beautiful. Only she who has experienced it can know what it is. Words are inadequate. Words are silly. How can you explain true ecstasy? Shaking and convulsing, I finally find out what a pussy is really for!

He is shirtless and yanking off his jeans when the waves ebb away. For a few seconds I simply lie there enjoying the show. He has an incredibly fit body. There is a beautiful tattoo on his left breast of a roaring tiger's face and a coiled snake on one of his biceps. I would have looked at them more closely, run

my tongue over them, but he pulls his boxers off and his dick springs out.

'Wow!' I exclaim, my eyes wide and an awed grin on my face. 'Huge and straight and beautiful.'

'It's all for you, babe,' he says cockily.

My heart lurches. 'Fuck me,' I whisper.

His eyebrows lift. 'I fucking intend to. For hours!'

'So, what you waiting for then?' I invite cheekily.

A slow, devastatingly sexy smile spreads across his face. He puts his knee on the mattress and comes toward me on his hands and knees. He has held back for much longer than I would have done, and now he is coming to claim his reward.

I lift my leg and rest the sole of my foot in the middle of his approaching chest. He freezes, a new flash of excitement in his eyes. He thought I was shy. But I'm not. I'll be the wild temptress he could never have suspected.

'My turn,' I say. 'My rules.'

I lift my body upwards and place my finger in the dimple made by the meeting of muscles in his shoulders. Without warning I grab his forearms and he lets me tackle him to the mattress. I push him down hard and sit astride his thighs.

Taking his erect cock in my hand, I toy with it, enjoying the way it jerks and pulsates in my palm. It has its own musky scent that steals deep into my mind, infuses itself as a

memory that will never be forgotten. Actually, it is a scent that drives me quite mad.

Like a feral animal, I bend my head and, taking him in my mouth, I suck the warm, satiny skin sensually and deeply. He growls, a low hum deep in his chest. The sound is erotic. I love blowing him. I lift my eyes and watch him watching his dick disappear into my face.

I slip the middle finger of my left hand into the slickness between my legs and sneak the finger between his legs up to his butthole. Michael, I remember clearly, absolutely adored it. I probe the entrance gently. A bundle of firm muscles pushes back. Nope, no one else has been in there.

Suddenly, a strong hand curls around my wrist and yanks it away. 'I ain't no pretty boy, baby. In my bed it's always going to be your ass that gets fucked.'

Right. Message received loud and clear.

And that, it seems, is the end of the 'my turn, my rules' episode. He fists his hand in my hair and thrusts his dick deep into my throat. Only once has a man ever done that to me and I was so shocked and offended I bit him. But with this god of a man, I'm not annoyed. Not even a bit. I let him take total control. He fucks my mouth forcefully. There's almost a desperation to his movements, a sentiment that I understand and welcome. It's good to know that at least on a physical level I'm as necessary to him as he is to me.

He reaches for something on the bedside table. I hear the sound of foil tearing. He passes the rubber to me. 'Climb on top of me,' he orders.

I roll the condom over his cock and hold myself poised over the massive throbbing shaft. The moment feels achingly sweet. The yearning to be totally filled is white hot. At a torturous snail's pace I allow his thick hardness to pierce into the wet heat between my legs and stretch me as I've never been before.

I stop the slow glide and hold myself suspended above him to accustom myself to his girth.

'An inch too far?' he growls.

'No, I can take it all. I know I can.' And I push myself down. Whoa! A shocked sound escapes and he smiles with satisfaction. As if it gives him pleasure to ruin me for all other men.

Our flesh slaps with a dull, wet sound while I impale myself on him over and over again. The faster I drop my sweat-slicked body over his shaft, the more heat collects between my legs.

'Harder,' he spurs me on, and lifts my body to speed me up.

My sex feels plump and tender with the pounding he is giving it. 'Damn your devil penis magic. I won't be able to walk for a week,' I gasp.

With muscles clenched, and the very devil in his eyes, he climaxes. Fascinated, I stare at him. He is a magnificent sight of pure maleness. He digs his fingers into my hips and, grabbing handfuls of flesh, he slides me on his body, agitating my clit until my juices flow over his cock and pool between us, and I break apart for the third time.

This orgasm is like brute force. It slams into me and I howl like a lunatic banshee.

When I return, breathless and with my hands gripping the sides of his chest, I see a fierce look shining in his eyes. I attempt to get off his body, but he holds on to me tightly.

'Not yet,' he says.

'No?'

'No,' he confirms, his eyes so hot and intense that heat crawls up my back and neck. I hope to hell he can't see it in the dark. To hide, I resort to being flippant. 'Say hello to the world's first ever dick warmer,' I croak.

He drags his thumb over my lower lip. 'Your lips are the color of ripe peaches, Savage.'

I lick my lips self-consciously. 'You're full of shit, Eden.'

He laughs. 'And your skin shimmers in the dark ... like pearls.'

'OK, now you're really taking the piss.'

He smiles. There is a new softness and a languor to his face that makes him so damn foxy I want to eat him with a spoon, but I

don't. The earlier cold shoulder from him still kinda hurts.

Still, it's not too long before he has me on my hands and knees. Gripping my buttocks hard he plunges into me all over again.

Dom

I drive into her like a man possessed. The room loses its solidity, and drifts away like a cloud. There is only her and me suspended in nothing. My mind spins and old magic circles around us. I lose all sense of time as her essence rushes through me, merging with me and revitalizing everything dead and diseased in my body.

Freezing cold waves still crash around me, but I do not feel the pain. I tighten my hold on her hips and roar like a beast. I know the pain will come back—its retreat is momentary—but the scale of the relief I experience is impossible to describe.

ELEVEN

Ella

You can forget so many evenings of sadness
For a morning of tenderness.
—Je sais, Jean Gabin

I wake up on my back with my cheek pressed against Dom's chest, his big palm resting on my belly, my feet entangled with his, a raging thirst, bursting for a pee, and a twenty-four carat bitch of a headache. My head is pounding so hard it hurts to even breathe.

Never again, I swear.

Gingerly, I lift his hand and, easing myself away from his heavy, warm bulk, I sit up at the edge of the bed. Separated from his body I immediately feel cold and hollow. Just the air conditioning turned up too high, I tell myself. I swing my legs to the cold ground. Ouch, my head. In the blue glow of the night light I make my way to the bathroom. Ohhhh

98

... Peeing hurts, too. With a long sigh I go into the kitchen in search of a glass of water. On the island top I see a black napkin with two painkillers neatly laid out next to a glass of water.

For a second I stare blankly at the sight.

He put it out for me!

I scratch my head. Ouch. I shuffle over to the napkin, pop the pills, down the water, and head back to bed. Very, very gently, because my head has now started throbbing hard enough to break, I slide back under the covers. A powerful arm circles my waist and a sleepy, warm voice murmurs in my hair, 'Sleep, sweet Ella. You'll feel better in the morning.'

Unable to speak, I close my eyes, and after a while I fall into a deep, dreamless sleep.

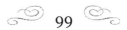

A sound wakes me up. I open my eyes, and Dom is sitting freshly showered and fully dressed by the bedside. His hair is still damp, and I am suddenly reminded of the first time I saw him. It feels like our first encounter happened a lifetime ago. Another era. He has become so much a part of my life.

'How are you feeling?' he asks.

I push hair out of my face and blink a few times. My eyes feel heavy and my mouth feels wooly. At least the headache is gone, though. 'I'll survive,' I mutter.

'Look, I have to go out, but stay as long as you like. Make yourself some breakfast. How about I take you out to lunch when I get back?'

'Uh, no, I can't stay. I've got to go to my mum's and then I'm meeting my best friend for lunch.'

'Right.' He takes his phone out of his pocket 'What's your mum's number?'

I stare at him, surprised. 'Why?'

He looks up from his phone. 'I'm a paranoid motherfucker. I always need next of kin information.'

Because I'm so startled by his arrogant assumption that I should give him my mother's number after two nights of ... hot sex—I guess that's what it was, there had been no lovemaking between us—I end up giving it to him. Besides, I'm not even properly awake. So this is officially an ambush of sorts.

'Now, your best friend's name and number?'

My eyes widen, but I cave in and give him Anna's number, too.

'Right, I'll get my driver to pick you up and take you wherever you want to go. He'll be waiting for you in the foyer.'

I shake my head. I just woke up and I'm being steamrolled into agreeing to all kinds of things. 'Please don't do that. I'll just call a taxi.'

'No you won't. Brian will take you,' he says, his jaw hardening.

I cover my eyes. It really is too early to fight with anyone, let alone a juggernaut like him. 'OK, fine.'

'I'll pick you up from your place at eight tonight. Wear your red dress.'

I uncover my eyes. 'Ah ... we're going out tonight?'

'It's Saturday. What else would we do?'

His phone must have buzzed in his pocket. He takes it, looks at it, and raises his eyebrow enquiringly at me. I shrug to indicate that he's welcome to take the call. He presses the button and listens to a woman's laughing voice saying something. I immediately turn my eyes away from him and pretend to be very interested in a ray of sunshine that's pouring in through the curtains, which he must have partially opened.

My stomach's churning with a mixture of hurt, shame and fury. What a sick bastard. As if he had to bloody take the call in front of me while I'm lying naked in his bed still smelling of sex with him. I don't let any of my feelings show on my face, though. He wants us to be enemies who fuck? Sure, I can do that. In the end, he'll be the one who's sorry. A voice in my head says, 'In your dreams he'll be the sorry one.'

'Cut it out, Layla,' he says into the phone and cuts the connection.

'What are you looking at?' he asks me.

'The dust motes,' I say softly, relief pouring through my veins. All is forgiven. He was talking to his sister. I feel gooey inside.

He turns his head to look at the particles suspended in the rays of sunlight. 'Why?'

'Because ...' I pause. Oh my God, I am so happy for no reason whatsoever. 'The dust motes are magic. They're around us all the time, but you can only see them in a burst of sunlight.'

'OK.'

'Don't you get it? They're the universe's way of telling us that there's more to life than we can see, hear or touch. You know, like dogs can hear things we can't, bats can feel sounds, and other animals can see ultraviolet light.'

He stares at me. 'And you're a tax collector?'

I shrug.

'I'm going, but before I go ...' He pulls at the sheet that I'm holding fast to my chest.

I clutch the sheet harder and laugh nervously. 'What are you doing?'

'Taking something to remind me of you.'

The sheet slips down my body.

'Open up,' he says, looking down at the triangle between my legs.

I spread my thighs and he inserts his finger into me. Unbelievable, but I'm already so wet that it just glides into me. He takes his finger out and sniffs it. 'That'll do me,' he says.

He kisses me on the mouth and then he's gone.

After the door shuts, I lie unmoving in the quiet of the empty apartment for a few seconds. Then I jump out of bed and run into the bathroom to see what I look like. I freeze with shock to see the state I'm in. Jesus! I've honestly never seen myself look more unattractive.

I shower, get back into my clothes and go downstairs. A man in a black jacket gets up from one of the sofas by the plate-glass windows.

'Miss Savage?'

'You're Brian?'

He smiles and nods. 'Where can I take you?'

I give him my address and he takes me home in a beautiful dark blue Bentley. As I get out of the back seat, the parking attendant who admired Dom's Maserati passes me.

'Does this one belong to the same guy?' he asks.

'Mmm,' I say, and, smiling like a cat who got the cream, run into my building.

My flat seems poor and cramped after his luxurious apartment. I quickly eat a bowl of cereal then take the Tube to my parents' home. My mother looks at me strangely.

'Are you all right, dear?'

'Yeah, why?'

'You just seem a bit pink. As if you're coming down with something.'

I cough. 'I'm fine, Mum.'

'Come through. I'll make us a cuppa.'

We have tea together, and I try my best to pay attention to my mother's chatter, but it's very hard going, and after a while I tell her I have to go meet Anna.

Anna and I meet in Starbucks. She peers at me closely. 'What's wrong with you?' she asks.

'Nothing's wrong with me,' I say with a sigh.

'You look like you're catching the flu or something,' she insists.

'OK. I slept with a man.'

'What the fuck?' she screams, so loudly the people at the next table give us a disapproving stare.

'Speak up, won't you? I don't think the people in the next street heard you,' I whisper fiercely.

'Tell me everything,' she orders, and takes a massive bite of her egg sandwich.

'There's not much to tell. He's just a guy. It's just a sex thing.'

'When do *you* do a sex thing?' she asks with her mouth full.

I grin at her. 'When he looks like a Greek god.'

'Who *is* this guy?'

'Someone we're meant to be investigating.'

Her mouth drops open and I see partially chewed egg and bread and something green. She swallows hurriedly and says, 'Jesus, Ella. Is this like the invasion of the body snatchers? You're sleeping with a tax dodger? You HATE tax cheats.'

I bite my lip. 'I don't know, Anna, I'm so confused. Everything I believed in for so long now seems like a badly thought out illusion. I can't explain it. All I know is I just have to be with him. He has something that pulls me to him.'

'Wow!'

'I know. Can you believe it? Me saying something like that?'

She shakes her head. 'So, it's serious?'

'No. There's no chance of that happening. He doesn't want anything more than sex from me.'

'What?' Her brow is furrowed.

'Yeah. He has walls like an impenetrable nuclear bunker. I think he's had some terrible tragedy happen to him. The first time we met, I walked in on him when he wasn't expecting me to, and he looked totally tormented. I have never seen anybody suffering in that way.'

'Not another fucking loser, like that psycho Michael.'

'He's not a loser. He's just had some kind of tragedy that he hasn't got over.'

'Oh no. You're going to fall for this guy, aren't you?'

'I won't.'

'You won't? You're already more than halfway there.'

'I'm not,' I insist firmly.

She sighs. 'Is the sex at least good?'

'Fan-fucking-tastic,' I say with a large grin.

TWELVE

Dom

She opens the door and my eyes widen.

I told my secretary, 'A red dress with a slit at the back.'

'How much do you want to spend?' she asked.

'Get her something spectacular that I'll enjoy taking off,' I said, and I never gave it a second thought after that. Until now!

Spectacular would be an understatement. She looks fucking unreal!

An innocent, but almost secret smile slips onto her face, and suddenly, for just a sliver of time, the past becomes the present. It is as if I have known her forever. Something in my gut catches, and I grab the tax investigator's hand and yank her hard. She tumbles into my arms in a delectable rush of soft flesh, blonde curls, and rising perfume.

Our bodies touching from chest to thigh, I curl my fingers into her silky hair and crush her mouth under mine. It parts. She tastes of chocolate. I plunder, I brand, I claim. Mine. This one's mine. Blood pounds into my dick. I want to walk her backwards into her flat, push her up against the wall, and shove my hard, hungry cock into her like on that first night.

I pull my mouth away, furious with my own lack of control.

She blinks up at me, dazed, panting, her spine tense. 'What's the matter?' she whispers.

I say the first thing that comes into my head. 'You taste of chocolate.'

'And that's a ... bad thing?'

'Ella ...' I begin, but there's nothing to say. I can't promise her anything. Give her anything. There is nothing for sweet Ella. Just these crazy moments until they, too, are gone. I shake my head. 'We'll be late. Let's go.'

She backs away from me. Her eyes are confused and hurt. 'Where are we going?' Her voice is pseudo breezy.

'My mate Justin is having a party.' My voice is distant. I hate the way it sounds, but it's too late to take it back.

She nods. 'That'll be nice.'

'You look beautiful.'

'Thank you,' she says sadly.

I'm fucking lame, I am.

Ella

I don't allow that strange 'episode' to spoil my night. I've always known that something is wrong, but I also know that it is neither of our faults. I'll just live for the moment, and let the future take care of itself.

The party is already in full swing when we arrive. Dom parks the car, and we walk toward the house. He doesn't hold my hand, or anything like that, but he keeps my body close to his so that it's clear to anybody looking that I'm with him.

The smell of a barbecue is coming from the garden, and Justin's living room has been turned into a giant disco with flashing lights. As we enter the room the DJ spins 'Feel This Moment' by Pitbull and Christina Aguilera, and it's as if they're singing to me.

'Ask for money and get advice,' Pitbull raps.

I turn toward Dom. 'I love Pitbull.'

'Yeah?'

'Yeah. You wanna dance?' I ask.

He looks down at me and suddenly grins. 'Why the fuck not?'

He pulls me to the middle of the floor, and, man, can he jive. I look into his sexy eyes and just for that moment I'm the luckiest girl alive. I laugh, feeling so happy. Oh, if only this moment could last and last ...

Justin is wearing a thick gold chain with a medallion and his shirt open down to his waist, and a couple of gangsta type gold rings, but he's cool. He raises his eyebrow at me. 'Now, why didn't I think of that?' he says. 'Wanna reduce your tax bill? Just get yourself a hot tax collector girlfriend!'

I just smile. This is a thin ice lake he's trying to get me to skate on.

'So, how much of a rebate are you givin' him?'

I shrug. 'Nothing.'

'Why not?'

'Tax cheats annoy her,' Dom says dryly.

'No kidding? Why?'

I shrug casually. 'I don't know. I guess it started when I was a kid. Some of the women on the estate sold Avon cosmetics in their spare time and never bothered to declare their earnings, so they always had extra to spend on nice things, and my mum and dad had everything taxed at source so we never, ever had enough.'

'Shouldn't that have made you decide to become an Avon lady?' Justin asks with a humorless laugh.

I search desperately for some kind of argument that will justify my views, but I can't find one, because within Justin's little joke gleams the real truth. A thing that has been polished by years of denial. My views about taxes have been shaped almost entirely by resentment and jealousy. I was jealous because my friends' **mothers** could afford better things for their families, and my mum couldn't.

Now, when I think about it, I realize, 'Good luck to them.' It wasn't as though they walked away with millions. They were just trying to make their families' lives a little better. If the government can afford a trillion to bail out banks, the little amounts they ferreted away couldn't have made any difference at all.

Unexpectedly, Dom comes to my rescue. He slips his hand around my waist. 'Ella couldn't be an Avon lady because she embodies a life of simple dignity, sacrifice and service.'

I stare at him, surprised.

Dom's cheeks slowly start to expand with a warm, radiant smile.

And I let out a long, inward sigh. He understands me.

Afterwards, we drink lots of cocktails, dance, and watch a fire-eater perform while we eat grilled jumbo prawns with a lime and garlic dressing. It's late when a fantastically handsome guy turns up. The photos I've seen of him on the net haven't done him a shred of justice. He's obviously very popular with the girls, because immediately there's a bevy of them around him. He looks over to us, catches my gaze, and a strange expression crosses his eyes. It passes in a flash. He comes up to us.

'When did the Inland Revenue start hiring ex-beauty queens to collect their taxes for them?' he asks with an irresistible sparkle in his laughing blue eyes.

Dom sighs heavily. 'Ella, meet my brother, Shane. Shane, Ella Savage.'

I hold out my hand, but he grabs it, and, pulling me toward him, envelops me in a bear hug. I'm so startled by his infectious warmth that I burst out laughing. He holds me around my waist and whispers into my ear, 'Has my brother managed to bring you over to the dark side?'

I giggle.

'We have chocolates,' he whispers darkly.

Dom reaches out, catches my wrist and tugs me firmly toward him. 'Haven't you got a bit of skirt you have to chase?' he asks his brother.

'Nope,' Shane says, and helps himself to a prawn from my plate. I realize I really like him. He must be the life of every party. He's such fun. As if on cue, a tanned blonde in a tight, hot-pink dress and seven-inch heels comes up to us.

'Hey, Dom,' she greets politely, smiles at me uninterestedly, and then bats her

eyelashes at Shane. 'You said I could have the first dance.'

'And I meant it,' he says, and, taking her hand, leads her towards the music. A few steps away he stops and turns back to me. 'You should come for lunch tomorrow. My ma makes a wicked Sunday lunch.' Then he's pulled away by the blonde. His departure leaves the air around us tense.

I sneak a look at Dom, and he's staring at me, his eyes wiped of all expression. 'Yeah, maybe you *should* come. Meet the rest of the family.'

'Maybe it's too early,' I say, giving him a chance to back out.

His eyes twinkle. 'We're gypsies, Ella. We're not subtle, and we don't do tact. We say what we mean, and we do what we say.'

I chew on my lip. 'Maybe we should wait until after Monday. Your family might hate me after my meeting with your accountant.'

'I don't care what happens on Monday. I could be dead by Monday,' he says flatly.

Before I can answer, there's the sound of a loud crash. Both of us turn to look. From where we're standing, I see Justin pointing his finger and arguing loudly with someone whose body language is just as aggressive. Beside him, on the patio floor, is an overturned chair.

'Shit, the Barberry brothers,' Dom says, jumping to his feet. 'Come on,' he urges and we walk quickly toward the brewing quarrel.

The men are arguing bitterly, their aggression quickly filling the air with tension. I can't properly make out what they are fighting about with all the onlookers shouting at the same time. As we arrive, it transpires that one of the Barberry brothers has insulted one of Justin's mates.

'I'll fucking kill you,' Justin is shouting to the Barberry brother who's supposed to have thrown the insult. There are four of them, and they all look as though they're spoiling for a fight.

Dom looks at me. 'Stay here,' he orders, and he strides toward the men.

I can see that the situation is quickly getting out of hand. And sure enough, seconds later someone throws a punch, and then it's a free-for-all. Everyone's swinging punches, chairs are being smashed, and more men are joining the melee. I stare at them in disbelief. I've never been to a party that's erupted into a steaming fight before. And it's a proper brawl, as well.

From the corner of my eye I see Shane wading in, coming to his brother's rescue. Not that Dom seems to be needing any help. He's roaring and going for it like a mad man. It's incredible how this party has disintegrated into this mess in the space of just a few seconds.

To my surprise, the other partygoers aren't trying to intervene and stop the fight, but are either watching it as though it's part of the entertainment, or clapping and

cheering on Justin and the Eden brothers against the Barberrys. There are four Barberry brothers against three, which seems unfair to me.

I see one of the Barberry brothers try to sneak in behind Dom and punch him from the back. Without thinking, moving purely on instinct, I pick up a wine bottle and, rushing forward, smash it over his head. There's a loud clunk. The man turns back with a growl and sinks slowly to the ground.

Ooops! In the movies, bottles that come into violent contact with human heads always shatter to smithereens. I look up from his prone body and meet Dom's eyes. There's a trickle of blood coming from his eyebrow, and he's staring at me with his mouth slightly open. I drop the bottle.

'He was going to hit you from the back. And that would have been unfair,' I say mechanically.

He grins suddenly, and it's like the sun has come out from behind a dark cloud.

'Behind you!' I scream.

Dom whirls around in time to face another fierce-looking Barberry brother. With my hand over my mouth, I watch Dom lay into him. As the man clutches his side and stumbles away, Shane walks up to Dom. The left side of his face is swollen.

'You OK?' he asks, as if it's the most normal thing in the world to turn up for a party and get into a massive punch-up.

'Yeah. You?'

He smiles. 'Always.'

Justin comes up to them and claps them both on the back in an almost congratulatory manner. He's laughing. This *is* normal for them! Dom leaves them and comes up to me. His eyes are dark and devouring. He looks at me as if I'm ... hmm ... well, food.

He grabs my hand and starts pulling me away. I run to keep up with his long strides.

'Where are we going?' I ask breathlessly.

'Somewhere I can ravish you.'

I grin. 'Dom, do you think he'll be all right?'

'Who?'

'The guy I hit with the bottle.'

'Are you kidding? It's gonna take far more than a bottle to down a Barberry boy,' he says.

And I laugh.

And so does he, as we run to the car.

We climb into it in a rush, and, like children who have been promised a trip to the ice cream parlor, we can hardly sit still with excitement. I smile a secret smile. It's clear that the rush of adrenalin and testosterone has fueled his sexual appetite and I'm going to reap the benefit. Dom drives us to a quiet country lane. And there, under a half-moon, he lays me across the back seat and buries himself all the way inside me in one hard slam, then works it until we're both an exhausted, satisfied, beautiful, sweaty mess. He reaches below, finds his trousers, rummages in one of the pockets and produces a gold bracelet.

'Here,' he says and capturing my hand fixes it on my wrist.

I bite my lip.

'What?' he asks.

'Did you steal it or something?' I ask with a grin.

'Why would you think that?'

'I don't know. Bracelets usually come in a box.'

'I can get you a box if you want.'

I shake my head slightly and gently touch the jewels on the pretty bracelet.

'Sapphires,' he says.

It's not big or flash and there is no great declaration that he bought them because they match my eyes or anything romantic like that, but I almost want to cry with happiness.

'It's beautiful. Thank you,' I choke

'You're welcome. Wear it all the time,' he says casually.

And my heart soars. 'I will.'

For a long time, we lie naked and as precious as the stars shining brightly in the night sky.

THIRTEEN

Dom

'**Y**ou wouldn't have any sisters for me, would you?' Shane teases Ella, a seductive smile spread across his face.

We're at my ma's for Sunday lunch. I don't know what I expected when I sprang Ella, the tax collector, on my family, but they've surprised me with the genuine warmth of their welcome. Never once has she been made to feel that anything might be amiss. Of course, Shane has to make a bigger ass of himself than usual.

'Afraid not,' Ella says with a grin. 'But I do have a brother if you're interested.'

'Ah, I'll let you know if I start batting for the other side,' Shane says with a laugh.

I know Shane's banter means nothing, but what the fuck! I feel jealousy pour through me. I place my hand possessively on her curvaceous bottom and throw my younger brother a 'back the hell off' glare.

With a brotherly pat on my shoulder and a mischievous glint in his eyes, he moves away.

Ella goes to join the women in the kitchen, and Jake comes over to me.

'So, that's Ella Savage,' he says quietly, a strange look in his eyes.

'Yeah,' I reply, my tone neutral but forbidding any further intrusions.

'She's beautiful.'

'I know.'

He raises his glass. 'Here's to you.' And for a moment there's a tinge of sadness in his face. Then Shane joins us.

'Hoi,' he says. 'What are you guys drinking to?'

'To Dom,' Jake says simply.

Shane grins wolfishly. 'And the *very* gorgeous Ella.'

I stare at him warningly, even though I know he's only yanking my chain. We all raise our glasses and drink. And I wonder if it has been a mistake to bring Ella to meet my family. They're ready for her, but I'm not.

Ella

I *love* Dom's family. And I don't say that facetiously. They're so kind, and I can feel how genuine their welcome is in every word and gesture. I especially warm to Layla. A laughing woman-child, she's the baby of the family. She throws her arms around me and kisses my cheeks as though we're long-lost sisters. It's immediately obvious that everyone loves her to death and is very protective of her.

Her husband, BJ, is another matter, though. He's the largest man I've ever met, with a hugely muscled chest and bulging arms. His eyes are so black it's impossible to know what he's thinking. He doesn't say much—his entire world seems to be made of his wife and their little boy. A highly energetic little thing who crawls around at frightening speed.

Jake, Dom's oldest brother, is the most mysterious of them all. I wouldn't want to mess with him. It seems as if he regards all the people gathered in that house as his personal responsibility. Almost as if he's the alpha and this is his pack. His wife, Lily, is

exotically beautiful and friendly, but not overly so. She's more reserved. His daughter is precocious, a cute little sweetheart whom I instantly fall in love with. We get on like a house on fire. Considering she's just three years old, I consider that a great victory.

I get a more muted reception from Dom's mum: outwardly kind and friendly, but sometimes I catch her looking at me warily. I guess I can't blame her. I'm the dreaded tax investigator. In some ways their kindness makes me feel like an impostor. Someone who's come to hurt one of them while enjoying their hospitality.

Shane was right—his mother's roast is wicked!

And thanks to Shane and Layla, lunch is a great laugh. I look at Dom, and realize I've never seen him as relaxed as he is with his family. He catches my eyes and smiles at me. A real, genuine smile.

After the meal, I join the women in the kitchen. Layla opens the freezer and brings out a tub of gin and tonic ice cream.

She looks at me and shakes her head. 'When I was pregnant I never had any cravings because I was so worried about my baby, but since I gave birth, I can't stop eating this stuff. I have it made specially. It's really delicious. Want some?'

'Uh, no,' I refuse politely.

'Just have a little taste,' she insists, coming to me with the spoon.

'No, really. I couldn't. I'm so full.'

 121

'OK. But if you change your mind, I keep a tub in Dom's house, too,' she offers with a smile.

'Thanks. I'll keep that in mind.'

While Layla stuffs the spoon of ice cream into her mouth, Lily pops her head behind Layla's and shakes it as if warning me never to try Layla's ice cream. Hiding a smile, I turn to Dom's mother. 'Can I do anything to help, Mrs. Eden?'

'No, child. Everything's already done. We all just come in here so my daughter can eat her ice cream.' She looks out of the window and then back at me. 'It's such a beautiful afternoon, I think we'll have coffee out on the terrace.'

I smile at her. How lucky this family is. I think of my poor parents stuck in their dark, poky flat and feel a little sad for them. And then Rob is in my head, saying how life is unfair. One child born with a golden spoon in its mouth, and another born starving.

'I really liked your family,' I tell Dom as we make our way back to London.

He glances at me. 'Yeah, I think they really liked you too.'

'I especially liked Layla. She's so sweet and childlike.'

'Hmm ... Don't be fooled. Underneath all that sweetness are nerves and determination made of solid steel.'

'Really?'

'Absolutely. She's very special.'

'You're really lucky to have them all.'

He doesn't turn to look at me. 'I know.'

There's silence for a few seconds, then he says, 'You never talk about your family.'

'I didn't think you'd be interested.'

His head swings around. 'Tell me about them.'

'Well, we're four: my parents, my brother and me. My parents live in London. My father took early retirement because he's plagued by all kinds of diseases, and my mother's his full-time caregiver. My brother's just graduated from uni and is now traveling around Asia with his girlfriend.'

He nods. 'Are you a close family?'

'I'm close to my parents, but my brother and I don't get on.'

'Why?'

'I don't like the way he treats Mum and Dad. They have so little, and he's constantly asking them for money.'

'Do they survive on their pension alone?'

'Not really. I help them with bits and pieces, groceries and stuff.'

His eyes swivel around. 'On your salary?'

I shrug. 'I manage.'

And again he looks at me as if he's
seeing me for the first time.

FOURTEEN

I have exactly three opportunities to trip up Nigel Broadstreet. Not because he sucks at his job—at full flow he is brilliant in a totally slippery way—but because of the things I have seen and heard while I've been with Dom.

However, I don't take them.

I just sit back and let Rob get more and more frustrated and lose more and more ground while Nigel puts forth more and more 'evidence' to support his claim that it was all an honest clerical mistake. No matter what Rob says or does, Nigel is impossible to faze. He is as cool as someone on a deckchair on the *Titanic* the day before the disaster, who had a helicopter ride off the ship that evening. Smooth. Confident. Secure. Unshakeable.

Watching Nigel in action isn't like watching a cheetah kill. There's no dazzling speed, claws, teeth, clouds of disturbed dust, or flying fur. It's more like watching a python wrapped around a goat. Every time the goat exhales, the python squeezes tighter until the last breath is gone. At which point the python, at its own leisure, swallows the goat whole.

As we leave the restaurant I pretend to be disappointed with the outcome even though I'm actually feeling very satisfied. It is rare that someone gets the better of Rob, and he's such a jumped-up, pompous ass that the pathetic side of me quite secretly enjoys seeing him brought down a peg.

In the car he fumes impotently. 'I hate these oily bastards. I'd love to investigate his accountancy firm. I'm sure there are more than a few skeletons rattling in there.'

Wisely, I say nothing.

As soon as I'm out of Rob's sight, I text Dom.

You might want to give your accountant a huge bonus this Christmas. X

I chat for a bit with the receptionist. She tells me her dog swallowed her ring so she has to dig through its poo with a stick. I make the appropriate noises of sympathy mixed with revulsion. When I leave her I take the lift upstairs and go straight to my desk.

I sit down and pull up the Integrated Compliance Environment (ICE) desktop

interface. I bring up the original search request I made for Lady Marmalade. Scanning through the form, I notice that, under 'Reason for Request and Any Additional Information', I've input all his brothers as additional associated persons that I wanted researched. Even BJ's name is there.

Leaning back, I gaze at the entry.

Every name on the list means something to me now. They're real people. They live, they breathe, they have hopes and dreams, they love their families, and they hurt when I go after them. I remember how emotionlessly I had compiled the list. How proud I used to be of the impressive responsibility I had, to make a decision on whether to challenge a declared tax return, and at what level that challenge should be made. How powerful it used to make me feel.

I was a different person then.

My mobile pings. I pick it up and look at it.

Want to celebrate with me?

I type back:

Obviously.

The answering ping is immediate.

Pick you up at 6. Wear a bikini under your clothes. Or don't.

Still smiling, I click out of the form and pull up the ICE Feedback Form. I complete it and click 'Send Form'. There. Case closed.

I sit for a while with my hands in my lap and then I open a fresh Word document and begin to type into it.

We drive out to his country house, which takes us about two hours. We turn off a main road and drive for another couple of minutes on a much narrower country lane before we come upon a rather nondescript steel gate, which he opens with the touch of a button on his key fob.

We then travel through about a mile of woods, which Dom tells me he has turned into a bee, bird and deer sanctuary. And as we drive slowly through, I start to see colorful birds everywhere.

'Oh my God,' I cry with delight, when Dom points out two sweet little deer hidden among the trees They do not scamper away, even at the monstrous sound of the V8 engine, but they gaze back at us, their large, moist eyes totally unafraid.

'Are they tame enough to be petted?' I ask, turning my head to stare at them.

'They come up to the house looking for food in the mornings. You can hand feed them then.'

'Really?'

'Yes, really,' he says and there is an indulgent look in his eyes. He obviously cares very much for his deer.

The sun is setting, but the air is still deliciously warm, and I'm almost struck dumb by the unspoilt beauty of the woods, and the thought that one man owns all this while people like me cannot even afford to buy a matchbox apartment. But I don't think these thoughts with the resentment I would have felt in the past. Instead, it is with a confused sadness. Is the world really just an unfair place where people have been arbitrarily made poor or rich by the accident of their birth? And does that mean that there is nothing I can do to make it a better place?

As we drive up to the house, I have to gasp. It is so beautiful. With two stately stone pillars and a frontage utterly covered in ivy, it is like an enchanted mansion straight out of a fairy tale.

Dom turns to me. 'Like it?'

'Like it? Dom, it's absolutely fabulous,' I enthuse. I turn to him. 'Does it remain empty while you are in London?'

'No, I have a housekeeper, and her husband doubles as the gardener. They stay the nights in the house when I'm not around, but when I'm here they live in that lodge there.' He points to a small cottage covered in wisteria and climbing roses. Nothing could be more English than that pretty little country home.

129

'Right,' I say, my eyes going back to the dreamy main house.

Dom parks the car and we cross the gravel and go up the stone steps. He pushes open the beautiful old doors.

'Don't you lock your doors?' I ask, surprised.

'Only in London.'

Inside are powder blue walls with white trims, gleaming oak floors, palladium windows with beautiful window seats, and a charming mixture of antique furniture and pastel furnishings. It is airy and elegant. There's a wingback chair next to a bay window and a book on a little round table next to it. I can almost see myself sitting in that chair reading and leaving the book there on the table.

I turn away from the sight. Disturbed. Why, I care not to think about.

He takes me through to a dining room with gold damask wallpaper and black and white curtains. It leads on to a large, shabby-chic style French kitchen with sandstone tiles. There's a cute breakfast table in a sunny corner.

'Want a drink?' he asks.

'I'll have some tea.'

He fills a kettle and sticks it on.

I sit on one of the chairs by the counter. 'Dom, I need to ask you a question. It's rather important to me, so please answer it as honestly as you can.'

He leans his hip against the island and glances at me warily. 'OK.'

'You think you shouldn't pay tax because the very richest are not paying theirs. But what would happen if everybody did that?'

He looks at me seriously. 'I wish everybody wouldn't pay. That would make this entire corrupt merry-go-round grind to a sudden halt. They can't imprison everybody and we'd then have to come up with something different. Not this corrupt system that has slowly concentrated half the world's wealth into the hands of one percent of the population and allowed eighty-five fucking people to amass as much as three and a half billion people combined!'

He pauses to let his words sink into my psyche.

Is he serious? My mind boggles. 'Eighty-five individuals own half the world's wealth! How is that even possible?'

'Not only is it possible, but the study concluded that soon the wealthiest one percent will own more than the rest of the world's population put together!'

I nibble the pad of my right thumb and reflect on his claim. It doesn't sound right. Too unbelievable. 'Where are you getting your figures from?'

He crosses his arms and narrows his eyes. 'It's public information, Ella. You can find it on the websites of the BBC, or *Forbes*, or the *New York Times*, or anywhere really.'

I scowl. How can this information be public knowledge and there still be programs on TV like *Benefit Street* where the poorest, neediest people are put to shame because they receive pitifully meager handouts from the government?

At that moment it occurs to me that not only have I watched these programs myself, but that I, too, have been hoodwinked into despising those poor people while the real culprits remained invisible to my rage and condemnation. What a clever sleight of hand by the one percent indeed!

The kettle boils and he pushes himself away from the counter, drops a tea bag into a mug and fills it with hot water. He looks at me. 'Milk? Sugar? Lemon?'

'Black, two sugars,' I say automatically.

He drops the cubes into the drink and brings the mug to me.

I smile up at him. 'You made me tea.'

He frowns and seems surprised. 'Actually, it's my first time, too. I don't believe I've ever made tea for anyone before.'

I put the mug down and reach into the purse slung across my body. 'I want to show you something,' I say. Unzipping it, I take out a folded piece of paper and give it to him. He takes it from me and unfolds it. I watch his eyes scan down my letter.

Then he looks up and smiles at me. It is a rich smile. 'You know, when we're at school, we're really only taught one thing that the system considers important. Every school

in the world has different curricula and different subjects, but all schools have this one agenda in common.'

'What's that?' I ask curiously.

'Schools tame children and teach them obedience.'

'Obedience?' I say slowly, tasting the word.

'Obedience to the bell, the teacher, the rules, the grading system, the uniform, the time-keeping. It's how the few control the many.' He re-folds my letter. 'This letter of resignation is your first act of disobedience. And for that I congratulate you.'

I look up at him, fascinated and intrigued. Never could I have imagined at first sight of this arrogant, cock-sure man that there was such hidden depth to him. 'Will the system ever get changed, Dom?'

He shrugs. 'I don't know, Ella. It's hard to fight it because it *is* us. *We* are the ones who are making this system work, with our apathy, our compliance, and our obedience.' He smiles and shakes my letter at me. 'But every time someone writes a letter like this, it gives me hope that one day, maybe not in my lifetime, but one day the world will be different.'

There's a sound at the kitchen door, and a middle-aged woman comes through. She has badly dyed blonde hair and a big smile on her face.

'Hello, Mr. Eden,' she greets cheerfully.

'Hey, Mrs. B. Come and say hello to Ella. Ella, this is my housekeeper, Mrs. Bienkowski.'

'Hi, Mrs. B. It's a pleasure to meet you.'

Mrs. B turns out to be a warm, bustling character. As soon as Dom disappears into his study to make some calls, she takes me upstairs to a huge master bedroom with floral curtains, cream carpets, and a massive bed full of pillows. She shows me how everything in the bathroom works and then she asks if I have any allergies. I tell her no and she tells me dinner will be at eight.

That evening we set off on one of the walking trails. The air is clean and there's no noise of traffic—only the sounds of birds in the trees. Everywhere there are feeding posts. A red squirrel races up a tree. At a water fountain a pair of courting pigeons are kissing and flirting with each other.

A feeling of peace like I've never experienced growing up and living in London steals into my body. I take large breaths of fresh air. We hardly speak because words are not necessary, and I think I'm too stunned by how much my life has changed. How much fuller and richer it is. How much I love him. There, I've said it. I love Dominic Eden.

I know he has promised me nothing, but oh, how I do love this man.

How could I not? He came into my life like a tornado. Inconvenient. Unwanted. Destructive. He overturns everything I thought I believed in and fills me with the kind of passion I never knew existed. So yes, I do love this complicated, damaged, rich, strange, kind, beautiful man.

I stop and he stops too, and looks down at me. In the last rays that filter through the trees and catch his face, he is beautiful beyond any prince I could have dreamed of as a child. I entwine my arms around his powerful neck, he dips his head and we kiss. The kiss is different. It is different because of me, because of where we are, and because of him, too. When he raises his head, his eyes are dark and enquiring.

I just smile mysteriously and carry on walking.

When we arrive back at the house, we eat in that country dining room with the black and white curtains. Mrs. B has lit candles. In their yellow glow Dom looks impossibly mysterious and romantic. When he smiles, my heart actually lurches. I truly cannot believe my luck. Here I am jobless, but so incredibly, unbelievably happy.

We have coffee out on the long terrace overlooking lush green lawns.

'Until you find another job, I want to take care of you,' he says suddenly.

'Thank you,' I say softly. 'But I'll be OK. I have a little bit put away for a rainy day.'

He touches my hand. 'Ella, it's not a rainy day while I'm around.'

Something in his statement jars, but I don't dwell on it. I'm living for the moment. The future is far off and could even be beautiful.

'I didn't mean to say rainy day. Honestly, I have savings I can dig into,' I say with a smile. I don't tell him that it is a pitifully small amount.

He looks at me intently. 'But I want to help, Ella. It will give me great pleasure.'

'How about I'll ask if I need help?'

He looks at me with a flash of irritation and I just laugh. He's cute even when he's annoyed.

Eventually, Mrs. B comes to say goodnight. We watch her toddle off down the path and disappear from sight when she turns at the side of the house. I lean back and breathe in the night-scented air.

'How quiet it is here,' I say.

'Mmmm' He turns his head to look at me. 'It won't be so quiet when I get a hold of you.'

I laugh, the sound rolling into the dark night.

He crooks a finger at me.

I point to my chest and widen my eyes as if to say, me?

He smiles slowly. 'Yeah, you with the gorgeous ass.'

I make a big production of sensuously uncrossing my legs and stretching my body out. I slink out of the recliner and glance at him from under my lashes. While keeping an eye on me, he is taking an ice cube out of his glass. Gosh. He really is one super-tasty dish. I actually can't wait to get to his skin. Can't wait for him to touch me, kiss me, take me. It's never been like this for me. Ever since I met him it as if I am in a dream world where only he and I exist.

I take my shoes off and the grass is springy and cool under my feet. When in an animal sanctuary... So I leave my independent, strong self in my handbag and getting on my hands and knees on the sweet-smelling grass, I slowly, and I mean slowly, cccccccccraaaaaawl to him. Yup, that's right. I will meet him animal to animal. Tonight is going to be a wild ride or my name is not Ella Savage.

I reach him purring like a tiger and angling my mouth I suck at the ice cube. Melted ice runs down my chin.

He puts his hand on my head and smiles. 'I don't like your pussy lower than my mouth.'

'No?'

'Fuck no.'

He grabs my hand and pulls me up. We run into the darkness of the garden.

'Where are we going?'

'Do you trust me?'

'Of course.'

'Good. Because it's time to face the truth.'

'What truth?' I ask breathlessly.

'There's a heated swimming pool at the bottom of the garden.'

I laugh. 'You're mad.'

'Totally.'

And I see it. A frosted glass structure. From the outside I can see many lights flickering in it. He opens the door and we are in. Lit purely by candles, hundreds of them, it is incredibly beautiful, with the wavy light reflecting on the water. It is also very warm. Like being in a tropical country. The candles are scented and the perfume is unfamiliar to me, but exotic, the way I imagine some jungle flower in the tropics to smell like.

'Wow! It's really hot in here,' I say.

He doesn't answer. He gets on with stripping me down to my bikini. I squeal when he picks me up and throws me into the deliciously warm water. I float on my back and watch him get naked before he plunges in.

He swims to me, wraps his arms around my body, and kisses me passionately. I have never kissed anybody while I am in water. It is a sensual, sinuous experience. When he lifts his head I am no longer in the middle of the pool, but have been brought close to an edge.

'Feel me,' he says.

My hands curl around his cock. 'Done,' I say.

And then I am slowly, with water sluicing down my body, rising out of the pool. Fuck! He's strong. I feel the hardness of the tiles by the side of the pool under my buttocks and thighs.

'I want to kiss your clit now...'

I spread my legs out eagerly. I've never known a man who is so crazy about eating my pussy as he is.

His lips move forward and kiss the front of my bikini bottom. Looking up at my face, he pulls on my hips to bring me even closer.

'Move the fucking material.'

Now that is what is called a fucking command. I pull the triangular piece of cloth slowly across to one side and expose my pussy to his eyes and lips. I put my hand on his shoulders to steady myself and press my naked pussy against his face.

'Lie back,' he orders.

With my legs still in the warm water I lie down on my back. I feel the cool tiles on my back and his cheeks brush against my thighs as he moves between them. My legs move up and across his shoulders. And so he licks. Long languorous, thorough licks. The same dedication with which way a dog would groom itself clean. Earnestly.

There's a job to be done here.

With each lick he goes deeper and deeper inside. One finger touches my hard clit.

'Oh!' I grab his head and spread my legs wider still. His tongue slips inside my pussy.

Just a bit. Wow! It is enough to carry me home. I moan when he uses his finger to gently spread open my swollen lips.

'So pink. So sweet,' he murmurs.

One finger slides inside as his tongue continues to lick. I push against the finger. It slides farther inside. My eyes close and my body arches. His finger moves in and out of my wet, wet pussy. He covers my clit with his mouth and sucks.

My hand is clenched on the tiny material that I am holding back. My body tenses and I begin to moan. He begins to rub his whole face in my pussy. The action is so dirty I explode right there and then. Gushing onto his chin and listening to him slurp my juices greedily.

I come up on my elbows. Breathing heavily and craving cock! 'I think I'm going to need a very big cock deep inside me.'

He grabs the sides of my bikini and yanks them down my legs. 'I agree.' He presses his palms on the edge of the pool and pulls himself out. Then he lays a towel beside me and I quickly get on my hands and knees, push my bottom up and wait.

His huge erection slides in slowly. The fit is tight and the sensation of being stretched and filled is wonderful. Then he holds still and my pussy calls him. I move against him, rocking my body, calling his sperm. This is the first time we are doing it bareback. Nothing between us, flesh to flesh. He reaches forward and starts massaging my clit. Little slow circles as I impale myself repeatedly on him. His stiff cock goes in and out of me like a piston.

'I'm nearly there,' I say, and he grabs my hips and rams into me. I gasp at the rough, hard slam. He fucks like a savage, jerking me like a doll. I feel his shaft become harder and bigger and then he sprays his load deep inside me. In seconds I am adding my own cum to his. It's a beautiful moment. We climaxed together. Without planning. Without trying. It just happened naturally.

He withdraws his throbbing cock and some of our warm cum gushes out of me, and drips down the inside of my thighs. He runs his fingers up and down my spine. We say nothing. We just enjoy the orgasmic high until we slip into warm water.

Like dolphins we glide and chase. Our bodies wet and slippery, we fuck in the water. I look deep into his eyes as I climax. He doesn't know it, but that is my body saying, I love you.

I don't know what lies in the future, and I don't care. I am just happy seizing the moment.

FIFTEEN

Ella

I return home the next day, still enchanted by the feel of deer eating directly from my outstretched palm, to find my answering machine blinking. One message at twelve thirty a.m. Who the hell left a message after midnight?

I press play and the message is blank. Well, it's not exactly blank—I can hear someone breathing. Frowning, I replay it. Yes, for at least thirty seconds someone held a phone to their ear and breathed into it. A chill runs up my spine. I dial 1471 and an automated voice says, 'Caller withheld their number.'

'Fuck you, Michael,' I whisper into the stillness of my flat.

I stand for a few moments looking at the phone. Then I pick up the receiver and call my mother.

'Hi, Mum,' I say brightly.

'Ella,' she says. 'Guess who I saw?'

'Who?'

'Your ex, Michael.'

I grip the phone harder. My mum doesn't know how much trouble I had with Michael. I never told her how crazy it all got because I didn't want to worry her. She only knows that he had become a pest and she was instructed to entertain neither phone calls nor any attempts from him to make contact.

I feel my heart rate increase. 'Oh?' I say as casually as I can. 'Where did you see him then?'

'I bumped into him at the supermarket.'

I frown. 'Which supermarket?'

'Morrisons.'

'You mean the small one near you?'

'Mmm.'

'Why was he shopping there? He doesn't live nearby,' I say, thinking aloud.

'I have no idea. He never said.'

'What did he say, then?'

'Not much. He was very friendly, though. He invited your dad and me for dinner. Obviously I said no. And then he went on his way.' My mother pauses. 'He didn't ask about you or anything like that.'

'When was this?'

'Day before yesterday. I wanted to tell you yesterday, but I forgot. I haven't done anything wrong, have I? I couldn't be rude.'

'Of course you didn't do anything wrong, Mum. But if you see him again, even accidentally, let me know, OK?'

'OK. When are you coming over?'

'This weekend?'

'That'll be nice. Why don't you stay the night?'

'Um … I probably won't. But I'll definitely come over on Saturday. We can do some shopping and then I'll take you and Dad out for lunch.'

'All right, love. Do you want to speak to your dad?'

'What's he doing?'

'What do you think he's doing?'

'Oh, if he's watching TV don't bother him. I'll see you both at the weekend,' I say quickly.

'Goodbye, love.'

'Speak later, Mum.'

I put the phone down and call Anna's office number.

'How was it last night?' she says with barely suppressed curiosity.

'Er … it was great.'

'Great?' she explodes dramatically. 'That's all I get?'

'I'll tell you all about it in one minute. Anna, has Michael tried to contact you?'

'Michael? I'm the last person that spineless, useless pig will call after the ear bashing I gave him the last time he tried to get *me* to pity *him*.'

'Right,' I say distractedly. Just the thought of having Michael in my life at this moment when everything is so wonderful and dreamlike gives me the shivers. I couldn't go through all that again.

'Why are you asking' Anna queries quietly.

'I think he called here last night, and Mum said she met him at the supermarket. I'm sure it's just a coincidence, but I just wanted to make sure he hasn't tried to contact you as well.'

'Coincidence? My ass! I'd call the pig right now if I were you and warn him that the injunction is still active. He's not allowed to come anywhere near you, or your family members.'

'Can I call you back Anna?'

'Sure. I'm here bored out of my mind. I'd love to hear about how you sucked Mr. Eden's fine, non-tax-paying cock.'

'Speak to you soon,' I say with a small laugh and cut the connection.

Right. Anna is right. The brightest thing to do is to face it head on and nip it in the bud. I dial Michael's number. Amazing how it's branded into my memory. I shudder at the thought that I'm again calling him.

The sound of his phone ringing echoes in my ear.

But he doesn't pick up, so I leave a coldly brutal message telling him to stay away from me, my mother, my workplace and all my friends. I remind him about the court injunction and tell him that if he ever calls me in the middle of the night again I'll get the police involved. Again!

I know he definitely won't want a repeat of what happened the last time.

I stand outside Rob's door holding my envelope, a tight ball of nervousness in the pit of my stomach. Well, you don't have to fear him after today. I knock on the wood

'Come,' he calls.

I open it and as I enter he looks up from some papers. There is slight frown on his face. 'What is it?' he asks impatiently.

I walk quickly to his desk and place my envelope down on his table.

He narrows his eyes. 'What's this?'

'It's my letter of resignation.'

His eyes pop open. For a second he actually looks panicked. 'What?' he erupts.

'I ... er ... I'm leaving HMRC.'

He stares at me with a shocked expression while I fidget uncomfortably. I certainly never expected this reaction. I've always suspected he secretly doesn't like me.

'Why?' he asks finally.

I look down at a spot on the blue carpet. 'We've actually had this conversation before, you know, about the unfairness of taxation. All this time, I thought I was making things better, but it turns out I'm not. I'm just perpetuating a system that is intrinsically wrong.'

'I see. So when did this change of heart come about?'

I shrug. I really don't want to discuss Dom with him especially since he dislikes him so intensely. 'It doesn't matter,' I say. 'I just came in here today to give you my letter in person and thank you for everything you've taught me. I won't be coming back after today. I've got some leave accrued to me and I'll just use it up as part of my notice.'

'Don't be stupid, Ella. No matter where you go there will always be unfair practices. At least here you know that you'll have a good pension scheme to take care of you.'

'Look, Sir. It's really kind of you to think of my future and everything, but I just can't stay.'

'But you're one of our rising stars. You have a real talent,' he says.

I look up, surprised by the compliment. I don't think I've ever had one from him. 'Thank you, Sir, for saying that. Er... it ... um ... means a lot to me, but my mind's made up. I just can't work here anymore.'

He frowns. 'Where will you go?'

I shrug again. 'I don't know yet. I'll probably find something temporary first and see how it goes.'

He holds my letter out to me. 'I'm not going to accept your resignation. It seems to me you are acting on an impulse. You should take some time to think about this more clearly.'

I don't take the letter from him. 'No, I have thought about it carefully.'

'You're throwing away a really good career on a whim. I always saw you as one of the managers here.'

He did! Really? Who would have guessed by the horrible way he treated me?

'It's not a whim, Sir.'

'Why don't you have dinner with me tonight?'

My eyes widen with shock. Wow, Rob has always been so distant and cold with me that I can't think of a more uncomfortable way to spend an evening. Besides I have absolutely nothing in common with him. I shake my head.

'It's not a date,' he says dryly.

I flush bright red with embarrassment. See, why I can't have dinner with a brute like him? 'I know that, Sir. Of course, it's not a date. I realize that you just want to try and talk me into staying, but really there's just no point. I've made up my mind.'

He stands. 'I think you're making a mistake.'

I smile awkwardly. It never crossed my mind that he would try to stop me from leaving that he even considered me such a valuable member of his team. Having said that, I suppose I was pretty useful to him. I did all the legwork so he could go out there and achieve all his monthly quotas.

'Why don't you take the leave that you are owed to relax and reflect on your

decision? And if for any reason you change your mind you can always come back.'

I shake my head and start backing away. 'No, my mind's made. Thank you, Sir, for everything.'

'Wait, Ella.'

Holding the door open I turn around and find he is only a few feet away from me. 'At least finish the bloody week,' he says angrily. 'You're going to leave everybody in the shit leaving like this.'

I'll be glad to see the back of him. I shake my head, and say resolutely, 'Goodbye, Sir.' Then I close the door, happy that I have made the right decision.

Three weeks later ...

SIXTEEN

Dom

My mother always has her children driving over to her other childrens' houses delivering homemade food. I'm sure she does it because she thinks it will mean we see more of each other. Maybe she's right. I suppose I would see less of them without these errands she makes us all run for her. This week I have a box of Shane's favorite—lemon cupcakes—sitting on the passenger seat of my car.

I turn off the engine, grab the cakes, and, locking the door, cross the courtyard toward his apartment. My brother is a funny guy. It's easy to misunderstand him and think he's a pushover or a shallow playboy, but that's just a façade he employs since it's so convenient and effective. The opposite is true.

He's actually very deep. Deeper than me, anyway. Me, I'm a simple guy. Neanderthal simple. Especially when it comes to women. My woman is my woman

and mine alone. Shane's more complicated. He doesn't go out there all guns blazing to keep his woman.

Like that time with Lily. It was Shane who was first interested in her, but he took her to a party at Jake's house, and Jake and Lily immediately hooked up. I know that Jake and Lily are mad about each other and all that, but the ease with which Shane allowed Jake to take his woman shocked me. I mean, I don't know what I would have done. I love my brother, but I might have had to punch him real hard. I know I definitely wouldn't have behaved like it was nothing, like I was some sort of wuss.

It bothered me so much that I asked Shane how he could be so cool about something like that. He shrugged and said, 'I can get a woman any time. Sometimes I open my kitchen drawer and one pops out. But I can never replace Jake. I'd give my life for him. He's family.'

And suddenly I remembered being fourteen again. My father had just been killed, and Jake had taken his place, so he was never in the house. It seemed to me then that my whole family was falling apart, and for some weird reason I became furious with my mother, as it was her fault that my father had stolen money from a gangster and had his throat cut.

Rebelliously, I began to act out. I cut school and would never come home until late, and when I did come home I wouldn't

speak to anyone. I was rude and sullen. I stole alcohol from the supermarket and got drunk. And when I was drunk, all I wanted to do was fight. I fought with everybody in those days.

Shane had just turned ten, then. One night I came home late, nearly midnight. Layla was asleep, Jake was out, of course, and only my mother and Shane were home. I walked into the house and heard a strange crooning sound coming from the living room. So I stopped and tiptoed to the door, and what I saw changed me forever.

My mother's head was in my brother's lap. She was weeping quietly, and he was gently stroking her cheek and kind of singing to her in a strange, reedy voice.

'Don't you worry, Ma. Don't you worry. Everything will work out perfectly. Jake and I'll take care of you. Dom will come around. He always does. Don't you worry, Ma. Don't you worry.'

I didn't show myself. I walked backwards out of the door. I went to an illegal, open-all-night pub and got totally smashed. I felt so ashamed. Shane had taken on the role that I should have. Jake was doing his bit, and I was slacking. No one had asked me to change my ways. Everybody was just waiting for me to come to my senses.

I woke up the next morning with an almighty hangover, and totally changed. I pulled my weight, and I've never forgotten the strength of character that Shane showed

at the tender age of ten. I know it's all still there. He's playing the part of the devil-may-care playboy, but one day the real Shane will come through and reveal himself.

I open the entrance door to the block of apartments. It's a Sunday night—the night porter is nowhere to be seen, and the reception area's deserted. I get into the lift and hit the button for Shane's floor. The doors open, I get out of the lift, walk down the short corridor, and knock on his door. He opens it in a stained T-shirt and ripped jeans.

'You OK?' he says.

'Yeah, good,' I reply and hold out the box of cakes.

'Thanks.' He takes the box, immediately opens it, and, selecting a cupcake, bites into it. 'Delicious,' he says, and holds the open box out to me.

'Nah,' I decline, and he shrugs and leads the way to his living room.

We get into the room, and to my surprise my niece and nephew are playing there. They squeal with delight when they see me.

'Where are their parents?' I ask.

'Mummy and Daddy and Uncle BJ and Aunty Layla have all gone to dinner,' Liliana announces importantly.

I look at Shane curiously. 'Are they here on their own with you?'

'What're you looking so surprised for?'

I cross my arms. 'They trust you to take care of their kids?'

 154

He seems amused. 'Yeah.'

I feel vaguely miffed. 'How come they never ask me to babysit?'

'They love their kids, Dom,' he says with a perfectly straight face.

I scowl. 'What the fuck is that supposed to mean?'

He raises both his hands in mock surrender. 'Hold your fire. Just kidding. It's probably because you don't know the first thing about babies.'

'How much is there to know?'

He grins. 'Can you change a diaper?'

Changing diapers! Of course not. 'Can you?' I ask, genuinely surprised. See what I mean about my brother being a dark horse.

He shrugs carelessly. 'Sure.'

'When did you learn to do that?'

'Had a girlfriend who had a kid,' he explains casually.

'How difficult is it?'

He pops the last bit of cake into his mouth and says, 'Piece of cake.'

'So why won't they trust me to babysit?'

He puts the box of cakes down on a cabinet and turns to me. There's a curious expression on his face. 'Do you want to?'

I look down at the kids and hesitate.

Shane begins to smile. That 'stupid, see, I knew you couldn't do it' smile.

It gets my back up. 'Yeah, I do,' I say nonchalantly.

'OK, I'll let you get on with it then.'

'Wait a minute. Where are you going?'

He looks at his watch. 'If I leave now, I could take Tanya out to dinner.'

I frown. 'You're going to leave them both here with me? Alone?'

'That's the plan. Unless you think ... you can't cope.'

I look at the children. They're sitting on the floor like two little angels. They stare back at me with big, curious eyes. Of course I can do it. What can possibly go wrong? If Shane can ...

'No, go ahead,' I tell Shane. 'Have fun. I can manage.'

But Shane has me figured pretty good. He's already pulling his T-shirt over his head and striding toward his bedroom. He comes back into the room in a clean T-shirt. My brother is so good-looking he doesn't even need to run a fucking brush through his hair.

'Right then,' he says cheerfully. 'All their stuff is in the spare bedroom. In an hour's time, warm the milk already prepared in the bottles and just give it to them.'

I nod slowly.

'You sure about this?'

'Have fun, Shane.'

'Laters,' he says to the kids, and, winking at me, goes out of the door.

I look at the kids. 'It's just us now,' I say, and walk to the window, where I watch Shane get into his car and roar off.

Inside the apartment Tommy gives a great big howl.

I rush to his side. 'What?'

'I pinched him,' Liliana confesses calmly.

'What did you do that for?'

'He poked me in the heart,' she says tearfully, pointing to the middle of her chest. 'And it hurt.'

'He's just a baby, Liliana. He didn't really mean it,' I explain reasonably.

'Yes, he did,' she insists as I pick Tommy up while he carries on with his meltdown. I realize immediately that there's a very bad smell coming from him. Holding him at arm's length, I then put him back on the floor.

Liliana is looking up at me with enormous accusing eyes, and I experience a rush of panic. I shouldn't have let Shane leave. I brush my face with my hand while Tommy continues to bawl inconsolably.

'Fuck it,' I mutter, and pick him up again. I hold him the way I see everybody else holding babies. The way Shane does. With his little stiff body close to mine—but he only screams even harder. I put him back on the floor.

'Do you want some ice cream?' I offer desperately.

Tommy stops crying instantly, and, standing up, gazes at me with tear-stained, hopeful eyes. His mouth is still quivering, just in case I don't come through with my offer. 'I cream,' he shouts happily.

'Yes, ice cream,' I repeat brightly.

157

'He's not allowed to have any,' Liliana forbids in an eerily grown-up voice.

At that, Tommy throws himself to the ground and howls his head off in frustration. 'I waaaaant i cream. I WAAAAANT I CREAM,' he hollers.

'Why is he not allowed ice cream?' I demand.

The little madam has her chubby arms crossed over her chest and is glaring up at me. 'Because we are *both* not allowed.'

'Why not?'

'There's sugar in it and sugar is bad for children.'

'Well, he's damn well having some,' I mutter.

'I'm telling,' she warns.

'Yeah, you do that,' I say, and, picking Tommy up by the armpits, begin to stride toward the kitchen with her following behind. If she's not careful she's getting Layla's disgusting gin and tonic ice cream.

There's a highchair pushed up against a wall. I drag it to the table and secure Tommy into it. The smell from his diaper is making me gag. I move away from him and open the freezer door. One scoop isn't going to kill them. Triumphantly, I pull out a tub of cookies and cream flavor and show it to Tommy.

'Mmmm,' I say in an exaggerated way and put it down on the counter.

Tommy cackles with delight.

I turn and look at Liliana. 'This is your last chance.'

She blinks, and I know I've got her.

'I won't tell if you won't,' I cajole softly. I know it's wrong to bribe her like this, but what the hell. This is an emergency.

She grins suddenly, and I see Jake in her little face. That same gorgeous smile. Something inside me knots up. I feel a wave of deep love for her.

'I cream,' Tommy demands, banging the tray.

'Right,' I say, and fill Tommy's bowl with three scoops of ice cream, because one just seems so mean.

I pull a chair out and raise my eyebrows at Liliana. Very primly, she walks over to the chair and slides in.

I put a bowl down in front of her. 'Do you know how to change a diaper, Liliana?'

She shakes her head solemnly. 'No, but Mummy knows how. We can call Mummy.'

I pick up the ice cream tub and start scooping it out. 'No. No, let's not.'

'Daddy knows how, too. We can call him,' is her next brilliant suggestion.

I put the tub of ice cream down. 'I know what,' I say in an unnaturally high voice. 'Shall we learn it together on the Internet after you finish eating your ice cream?'

She starts bouncing up and down. 'OK.'

I get my phone out and dial up YouTube—how to get a diaper on a baby in less than one minute. I put my phone on the

table and we watch the video together while Tommy spreads ice cream all over his face, clothes, and chair.

When it's over, I look across at Liliana. 'You ready?'

I pull a couple of kitchen towels, and as I'm walking toward Tommy, he manages to spin his bowl and it flies in the air and crashes dramatically to the ground, breaking and spilling ice cream everywhere. Christ! Liliana covers her mouth with both her hands. Over her hands, her eyes are round and full of an 'oh, oh, look what you've let happen now' expression.

'Want i cream,' Tommy bawls.

Jesus. This is turning out to be much harder than it looked.

Liliana uncovers her mouth. 'Uncle Shane always uses Tommy's plastic bowl.'

'Great. Thanks for the early tip,' I mutter.

I stop for a moment. I need to think. And I can't think with all this noise. These kids are doing my head in. First: stop that kid from howling. He wants ice cream. She says plastic bowl. Right.

Ice cream.

Plastic bowl.

I open the cupboard and find a green plastic bowl. I show the kid the bowl and he stops howling. I toss a couple of scoops into it and plonk it in front of him. He sticks his spoon into it and shovels it into his mouth.

'He'll be sick,' a small, knowing voice says.

'No he won't,' I snarl.

'You shouted at me, Uncle Dom.' Her lower lip starts trembling.

Oh no. Oh no. 'No I didn't,' I deny, while plastering a big, fake smile on my face.

'Yes, you did,' she wails and scrunches up her face.

For fuck's sake! I start walking toward her. 'That was just a joke, sweetie. I wasn't shouting. Look, do you want more ice cream?'

She sniffs and nods.

I grab the tub and put four generous scoops into her bowl. I look at her, and she stares at me with her spoon lifted meaningfully above her bowl.

'More?' I ask incredulously. This is the drama queen who claimed sugar is bad for children.

She nods vigorously.

I don't believe this. I throw another couple of scoops in.

'Thank you, Uncle Dom,' she says solemnly, and drops her spoon into the ice cream. While they're eating, I pick up the broken pieces from the floor. The ice cream is melting fast, but I manage to mop up the largest blobs with paper towels. However, I can see that I'm going to have to settle them in the other room and come back to clean this mess.

SEVENTEEN

Dom

After they've eaten, I clean Tommy's face and hands, pick him up, and, with Liliana following behind, carry him to the spare room. It's a surprise to see it done up colorfully with two cots in it. They must stay with Shane often.

I put Tommy on his back on the table with the plastic mat spread on its surface.

Liliana wrinkles her nose. 'Tommy stinks.'

'You bet he does.'

There's a pile of nappies, and I take one and unfold it, and place it on the table. I undo the straps on the sides of Tommy's diaper and lift the front flap away from his tummy. The sight and stench of the kid's shit just makes me want to gag. I mean, seriously gag. I actually start to retch. And I would have been sick too if I'd not very quickly re-closed the diaper and taped it back on.

'That's not how you change it,' Liliana says.

'I know that,' I say, turning my head to the side and taking deep breaths of clean air. I pick up my phone and dial Ella's number.

She answers on the third ring. 'Hey, sexy,' she breathes into the phone.

Not feeling sexy right now. 'How do you feel about changing a very smelly diaper?'

'Um ... Is this a trick question?'

'No.'

'It sounds like one.'

'Look, I need to change a diaper, and I can't get past the gag reflex.'

She begins to chuckle. 'I'll be right over. Where are you?'

'I'm at Shane's apartment. I'll text you the address.'

My phone rings again. It's Lily. Oh fuck! 'Hey, Lily,' I say too brightly.

'Hey, Dom. Shane called to tell us you've taken over. How's it going?' she asks casually, but I can hear the thread of panic in her voice.

'Great.'

'Yeah?'

'Yeah,' I insist confidently.

'Er ... Can I speak to my daughter, please?'

'Sure,' I say, and, looking at Liliana, put my finger on my lips to warn her not to say anything about the ice cream.

She nods conspiratorially. I smile at her approvingly and show her the thumbs-up signal.

She takes the phone, listens for a moment, then says, 'Yeah, but Uncle Dom gave us ice cream. Tommy had some, but I didn't have any.'

I stare at the little lying rat in shock. What a bare-faced liar! She drops me in the shit and saves her own skin. Even I wouldn't have lied like that at her age. Hell, her belly is still stuffed full of undigested ice cream.

'And, Mummy'—she looks up at me before continuing sanctimoniously—'Tommy's diaper is full of poop, but Uncle Dom doesn't know how to change nappies. He called someone to come and help him.' She listens for a bit more then she says, 'Nope. Nope. OK, Mummy. I love you too, too much too.' The little minx then hands the phone back to me. 'Mummy wants to speak to you.'

I bet she fucking does. You little rat, you. I glare at her as I snatch the phone from her.

'Hi, Lily.'

'Is Ella coming round, Dom?' Lily asks crisply.

Bloody hell. She's sharp. 'Yeah,' I admit.

'Oh! Good ... er ... when?'

'Fifteen minutes tops.'

'That's fine, then. We'll be back in an hour's time. Is that OK?'

'Yeah, that's just fantastic.'

'See you later. Oh, and, Dom … Don't give my daughter any more ice cream,' she says, and I can fucking hear the laughter in her voice.

'Not a drop,' I say, and kill the call.

'Is my Mummy mad at you?' Liliana asks innocently.

Un-fucking-believable. 'What do you think, you little troublemaker, you?' I ask as my phone goes again. I glance down. It's Layla. I groan. Now what?

'Hey, Layla.'

'Dom, where's my son right now?'

I turn around to where I saw him last, and to my horror he is nowhere to be seen. I feel a flash of panic. The flat is eerily silent.

'Oh fuck,' I curse.

Layla's voice is deliberately calm. 'He'll be in the kitchen, Dom.' I start running toward the kitchen. Layla is right. He is. He's sitting by the bowl of cat food. And … Oh! Damn! He's fucking scooping up handfuls and *eating* it.

'I found him,' I say, lifting him up with my other hand.

'What's he doing?' Layla asks.

'Nothing,' I say, as I stuff him into the highchair.

'What did you call for, Layla?' I ask, while I try to hook pieces of cat biscuit out of Tommy's mouth.

'Just to tell you to put the cat bowl up where Tommy can't reach it.'

'Yeah. I'll definitely do that.'

'Call me if you're unclear about anything, OK?'

'Right, will do.'

'Bye.'

I press the disconnect button and throw my phone on the table. Jesus, kids and their crap. How do people put up with this shit? I clean his mouth out while he tries his best to swallow the brown mush down. I wipe his hands.

'Uncle Shane doesn't allow Tommy in the kitchen because he likes eating the cat's food,' Little Miss Perfect says.

'Yeah?' I have a new respect for Shane. I had no idea kids were such a handful.

'You have to watch him or he'll drink out of the toilet, too,' Liliana chirps, nodding her head sagely.

I turn to look at her. She's enjoying this. Well, she's not going to win. A fighter can't be afraid of anything.

I pick up the cat bowl from the floor and put it on the counter. Then I lift Tommy up and stalk into the living room. The truth is, I feel quite distraught. I don't know if cat food will make the kid sick. I put him on the floor. I want to Google the effects of eating cat food, and I realize my phone is still in the kitchen. I go to get it, and come back to find Liliana standing in the middle of the room with her hands on her hips.

'Tommy is sucking the cat's tail,' she announces in what can only be described as a passive-aggressive tone.

'What the hell?' I turn to look at Tommy, and indeed he's sucking on its tail. I run to him, pick him up, and try to shoo the cat away, but it hisses at me and refuses to move. I drop Tommy onto the sofa. There's a toy train on the table and I give it to him. He takes it with a squeal of delight. How much longer before Ella gets here? I really can't handle this for many more minutes. I run my hands through my hair.

'I'm bored,' Liliana says.

I rub my hands together with fake enthusiasm. 'So, what shall we do until Aunty Ella comes, huh?'

Liliana shrugs. 'Shall we play hide and seek?'

'Nope. Let's not do that. How about we watch some TV?'

'OK,' she says agreeably.

'Lee Jaw,' Tommy says.

'What?'

'Little Lucien,' Liliana translates.

I switch on the TV, find the video, and press play. Both kids settle on the floor. The doorbell goes. Oh! Thank God. I rush to open the door and by God Ella is a sight for sore eyes.

'Hey, sexy,' I say looking her up and down. To my horror, I see Tommy shoot out of the front door past my legs. Honestly, I'm way too shocked to do anything, but Ella catches him by the scruff of his T-shirt.

She smiles at me. 'When they run away from you, they're not really running away. They just want to be caught.'

'Oh, boy, am I glad to see you.'

I pull her in and close the door. 'Listen, Ella. Tommy ate a bit of cat food before I could get to him.'

To my relief she grins. 'It won't hurt him. Most things won't. Kids are made to be as tough as old boots. To ensure the survival of the human race and all that.'

'Really?'

'Yeah. My brother took a dead cockroach from the mouth of a cat and ate it. My mother never recovered, but he was perfectly fine.'

I sigh with relief. 'Christ was tested in the desert by Satan. I've been tested by my nephew.'

EIGHTEEN

I walk into the kitchen and catch Dom on his hands and knees wiping a wet sponge on the floor in circles, an action that is only serving to smear melted ice cream all over the floor. I stand there looking at him, at his endearing helplessness, and falling in love all over again. I don't know how annoying an undomesticated male can eventually become, but right now, it's like watching puppies fall asleep on the lip of their food bowls. Cute, cute, cute.

He looks up, sees me, and sudden panic flares in his eyes.

'Where's Tommy?' he asks urgently.

'Relax. He's *inside* his playpen with a bottle of milk.'

I hear him exhale with relief.

'And Little Miss Perfect?'

I bite back a smile. 'Watching a cartoon.'

'Is it normal for a three-year-old kid to talk like her?'

'She is a bit precocious, but kids nowadays are more advanced than we were.'

'Right,' he mutters.

I smile at him.

'Thank you,' he says.

I start walking toward him. 'Need some help?'

'Nah, I think I've nearly got it all,' he says, looking down at the mess.

I go over to the cupboard under the sink, and, opening it, find some cloths and a bottle of floor cleaner. I find a bowl and fill it from the hot water tap. I squirt a little cleaner into the bowl and walk over to him. I take the sponge out of his hand and replace it with a wet cloth. I toss the sponge across the room into the sink and squat beside him. I wink and begin to clean the floor. He copies my actions exactly.

'So you got the diaper on, huh?' he asks casually.

'Yeah.' I dip the cloth into the bowl of warm water and rinse it.

'Any problems?'

'Nope.'

'Hmmm ... Good.'

There is silence for a few minutes.

'What do you think they feed that kid?' he asks.

I hide my amusement as I wring milky water out of the cloth. 'I don't know. Maybe dead cats.'

'I never imagined a baby could stink like that,' he says in an awed voice. He actually shudders.

I push the bowl over to him. 'I'll have to be sure not to fart in bed, then.'

He stops swirling the cloth in the water. 'Let's make a deal. Any time you eat a dead cat for dinner, and you think you're gonna fart in bed, just let me know, and I'll put a sick bowl by my side,' he says very seriously.

I laugh so hard at the thought of him puking his guts into a bowl that I fall over backwards. He sits on his heels looking down at me. 'Have I ever told you, Ella Savage, you are one delicious woman?'

'Is it because I'm covered in ice cream?' I giggle.

He bends down and kisses my nose. 'Even before that. Well before that,' he growls.

We're interrupted by an incoherent scream of rage coming from the living room. Dom freezes.

'Go on,' I say. 'I'll finish up here and join you.'

'No, you go. I'll finish up here and join *you*.'

I try not to chuckle. 'Are you afraid of them, Dominic Eden?'

'Terrified,' he says.

I kiss his nose and go into the living room. Tommy is upset because Liliana has changed the channel.

'Right,' I say. 'No more TV. How about we read a book?'

Both are happy with that, so I take Tommy out of the playpen, and together we choose a book and cuddle up on the sofa to read it. By the time Dom comes in, both kids are leaning on either side of me and we are more than halfway through the book.

He stops at the entrance and watches for a minute before he comes in and sits down with us. After reading the book, we play with the kids.

It's a game where Dom has to say, 'Fe fi fo fum, I smell the blood of a half-gypsy girl and the blood of a full-gypsy boy.'

Total panic ensues, with Dom taking on the persona of a zombie-like creature and chasing the kids, and them dodging his flailing arms while they squeal, scream, and laugh hysterically. As soon as their parents arrive, Liliana dashes to the door and lunges at her father.

'Tommy broke a bowl, Daddy,' Liliana says, as soon as she is high up in her father's arms.

'I smell ice cream,' her father says with a straight face.

She covers her mouth. 'Tommy ate ice cream.'

'And you didn't?'

She shakes her head vigorously.

Jake looks at me. 'My daughter is such a liar.'

'You can say that again,' Dom mutters.

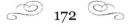

'Why does my son smell of cat food, Uncle Dom?' Layla asks.

Dom coughs.

'Because Uncle Dom let Tommy eat cat food,' Liliana says.

'How much?' Layla wonders.

'Maybe one mouthful,' Dom admits sheepishly.

Layla grins. 'Actually, I think you coped brilliantly. Much better than I thought. What are you doing next Sunday?'

Dom actually takes a backward step, and everybody laughs. Even BJ joins in at the terror on Dom's face.

After they've gone, Dom closes the door and turns to me. 'Do you want to have sex in my brother's flat?'

'No, I don't. But you can take me to dinner and then have sex with me at my place. You won't believe what I'm wearing underneath these boring old clothes.'

His eyes brighten. 'What are you wearing?'

'It's a surprise.'

'Let's go,' he says, and bundles me quickly out of the apartment.

NINETEEN

'I'll go feed the parking meter,' I offer, opening my bag and getting my coin purse out.

'No, stay in the car. I'll do it,' Dom says.

I shake my head. 'Dom, it's just there across the road. I'll do it,' I insist, and, opening the passenger door, get out.

I cross the road, put enough coins into the machine for two hours of parking time, and get a receipt. When I look up, I see that he has got out of the car and has his forearms resting on the roof as he stands looking at me. A breeze blows at his hair and he smoothes it down. He is so gorgeous I still get butterflies in my tummy just looking at him.

I grin at him and step onto the road. There's a loud blare from someone's horn, and I wake up from my little dream world where only Dom and I exist. I turn my head and see a white van coming, so I quickly step back onto the pavement.

The van passes, and Dom comes back into my sight, no longer casually resting his forearms on the roof of his car, but standing with his hands at his sides and staring at me in disbelief. His face is white and his mouth is hanging open.

'What?' I mouth, shaking my head.

A car goes past. The road becomes empty and I run across it.

'What?' I ask again.

He shakes his head slowly, blankly. 'Nothing.'

'You're as white as a sheet.'

He looks at me strangely. 'Am I?'

'Yes.'

'I thought that car was going to hit you.'

I laugh. It's not really a proper laugh. I'm disturbed by the sudden change in him. His expression and demeanor are so bizarre and out of character. We were laughing two minutes ago. 'Well, it didn't,' I say.

'I know. I saw that,' he says robotically.

'Dom, it wasn't even a near miss. I had plenty of time.'

'I know,' he says again.

I take his hand, and I'm shocked to find it trembling.

'What's the matter, Dom?' I ask urgently.

'Nothing. Let's go to dinner.'

I give him the parking receipt and he displays it on the dashboard and locks the

car. Then we walk to the restaurant and sit opposite each other. I look at him and he looks away.

'Dom, what the hell is going on?'

He turns to me. 'Leave it alone. Please.'

Because I can see that he is so extremely affected, I drop it quietly.

The waitress comes and he orders a triple whiskey. My eyebrows rise involuntarily, but I say nothing. When the drinks come, he downs his in one go and calls for another.

We order our food. It comes and we eat. All the while, we talk in a wooden manner. He tells me Lily is pregnant. She just found out today. Shane has started dating a magician called Tanya. Jake is sending their mother on holiday to Spain. And I tell him my mother has invited us to dinner on Saturday. He nods. He smiles. But his face is a mask.

Dessert menus are flourished. He wants nothing. So I follow his lead. He refuses coffee. And then I know he doesn't want to spend any more time with me.

He's pushing me away.

And it hurts like mad. Why? What have I done? How can he just shut me out for no reason like this? I start to feel angry, but I'm unable to express my anger. Some part of me knows that whatever it is, it's serious. It's eating him up. The bill gets paid.

'Come, I'll take you home,' he says, getting to his feet.

I nod and pick up my purse. Yes, he definitely wants to get rid of me. We walk to the car in silence. We drive in silence. Outside my apartment, I turn toward him.

'I'll call you tomorrow,' I say quietly.

'Yeah, OK.'

He bends and kisses me lightly on the cheek. 'Goodnight.'

He's dismissing me as if I'm some woman he doesn't give a shit about. I feel utterly abandoned. I peer into his closed face. 'Have I done something wrong, Dom?'

He shakes his head. 'No, it's not you.' And then he grips the steering wheel. 'It's not you,' he says again. As if in those three words lies the solution to what is eating him.

'Goodnight,' I say.

'Goodnight, Ella,' he says softly.

I get out of the car, sad and confused. He waits until I get into the door of my apartment building before he drives off. I lean against the wall of the foyer and listen to his car blast off into the night before I slowly climb the stairs up to my flat. I let myself in. There is a lamp burning in the living room. I walk to the sofa and sink heavily into it. It feels as if my whole world has just collapsed.

I'm in love with a man I cannot understand. A man who is closed off to me. The only time he's real with me is when we're in bed, but tonight, for no reason that I can see, he has rejected even that from me.

I *know* we have something.

It feels so real, but is it enough?

I go into my bedroom and sit in front of my dressing table. My face looks dazed and lost and I feel like crying, but I don't. I tell myself that I am strong. I can be strong for him and for me.

One day he will tell me what's wrong.

One day I will make his demons go away. Until that day, I will be here waiting and loving him. I cleanse my face, get into my pajamas, and finish my toilette. Then I go back into the living room and listen to music.

I listen to Heart singing 'Stairway to Heaven'. And the sadness of the song makes me tear up. The song ends, and my phone buzzes. A message from Dom. I am so desperate to open the message that I drop the phone. I pick it up and click on the text.

Are you still up?

My hands shake as I type in my one word reply: Yes. And click send. I cover my mouth and wait. The phone sounds again almost immediately.

Don't go 2 bed. Coming round in 10 minutes.

I stare at it. And suddenly it's as if I've been told I've won the lottery. I leap up from the sofa and run to the bedroom. I get out of my PJs and slip into a sexy nightie. It's see-through with a plunging neckline and little pearl buttons. I light some scented beeswax candles. I slick on nude lip gloss. Standing in front of the mirror, I brush my hair and dab perfume onto my wrists.

Once I'm satisfied with my appearance, I go back to the living room and because I gave him a key to my flat last week I arrange myself in a sexy pose on the sofa. I hear his key in the door and hurriedly fluff my hair. The door opens. He stands for a moment in the doorway and sways slightly. Then he comes in and, closing the door, leans against it. I stare at him. He is dead drunk!

'Hey there, tiger,' he drawls.

'Hey, you,' I say cautiously.

He starts walking toward me, stumbles once, rights himself, and continues on his journey to me.

'You drove here like this?' I ask incredulously.

He nods.

'God! Dom. You can barely stand. You could have killed yourself. Or someone else.'

'I didn't,' he mutters, 'kill anyone, if that's what you're worried about.'

I stand. 'I'll make some coffee for you,' I say, heading toward the kitchen. I love him, but I'm not going to condone drink driving. As I pass him, his hand shoots out and he pulls me into his hard body.

'I spent a lot of time and money to get into this state. I don't want to sober up just yet, thanks,' he says.

I look into his eyes. There's no real focus in them. If I'm going to find out anything, now is the best time. 'OK. Come sit with me and let's talk.'

He shakes his head slowly. 'I didn't get this way to sit and talk with you.'

'What do you want to do, Dom?'

'What I always want to do when I'm around you, Ella.'

A chill comes into my body. Here. Cold, clear proof that I am nothing but a good fuck. I'm in love with the guy, and all he wants from me is sex.

'Is that all you want from me?'

He frowns and peers at me. 'Awww, Ella. We have this. Isn't this good?'

I don't answer him.

'C'mon, babe. Don't kick a man when he's down.'

'Are you down?'

He breathes out. 'Like you wouldn't believe.'

'What's wrong? Tell me, please?'

'You don't want to know.'

I stare at him with frustration. 'But I do.'

'Trust me, you don't want to know.'

I look up at him, confused and intrigued. What on earth could it be that I wouldn't want to know?

He frowns again. 'I can't talk about it yet,' he says and slips his forefinger into my cleavage. He gazes into my eyes. 'You're so beautiful,' he whispers.

In the candlelight, his eyes glimmer. The air is snatched from my throat. I suck in

a breath. Strains of music surround us. It's so sweet and intoxicating, it should have been magic, but it's not. An air of barely suppressed grief hangs around him. He sighs heavily, and a deep worry line etches itself between his eyebrows.

My heart feels heavy.

'There are all kinds of memories hiding in the curves of your breasts,' he murmurs. His eyes flutter shut and then snap open. He is maudlin. Vulnerable.

His other hand comes up and cups my breast. He rolls my nipple between his fingers and I feel the familiar itching between my legs start. His eyes darken as he thrusts his knee between my thighs. I push my sex against the hard muscles and feel his cock pressing against my hip, straining to get to my wet heat.

'Oh, Ella,' he groans, and, lifting me up, clumsily carries me to my bed.

He drops me on the bed, and, with haphazard urgency, removes his shoes and clothes. He lands on the bed heavily and immediately rolls onto his back.

'Ride me. I want to watch your face when that hot little pussy of yours stretches wide for my cock,' he growls.

I clamber over him and sit on his thighs.

He pops the two little pearl buttons on my nightie. My breasts spill out and he slides his hands over the flesh and massages them.

'You really are so ripe and beautiful,' he mutters to himself.

I arch my back to push my breasts into his hands.

'Get naked,' he orders.

I pull my nightie over my head and fling it to the floor.

He takes a deep, satisfied breath, curls his hands around my midriff, and pulls me down for a kiss. I spread myself flat over his hardness as his mouth claims mine. He smells of alcohol and something broken. I don't know him, and he won't allow me in. The thought is extraordinarily painful. A lone finger strokes the swollen lips of my vulva as the kiss goes on. It makes me melt into him until he digs his fingers into my hips. I pull away from his mouth and stare down at him.

'Come, sit on my face,' he invites.

I knee-walk along his body and turn to face his feet. Hovering over his face, I slither and snake my body like a belly dancer so he can see what a gooey puddle my pussy has become.

'So eager, so wanton,' he growls.

Cupping the globes of my bottom as I gyrate teasingly above him, he lifts his face and extends his tongue. It flicks my clit and I whimper with the velvet heat. He pulls me lower and lets his tongue worm its way through the damp undergrowth.

As soon as he tastes my syrup, he pulls me all the way down, and I helpfully spread my thighs as wide as I can. I reach down and

let the tip of my tongue flick and tickle his cock. He shudders under me and glues my vulva to his face. I feel my juices flow out of me and drip into his mouth.

Down his throat they go.

Fisting the base of his shaft, I take the meaty pillar deeper into my mouth, curling my tongue around it. I bob up and down, my eyes shut. The rest of the world melts into nothing. There is only his mouth on my pussy and his cock in my mouth.

My orgasm comes suddenly, without warning. I push my palms into the mattress and climax hard with his cock buried deep in my throat, my nipples throbbing and tingling, and my whole body singing.

In all the rush and uproar, it occurs to me that I am hopelessly addicted to him. That I've been addicted from that first fix, when he threw me against a wall and shoved his cock into me without asking my permission.

A drop of slippery liquid touches the roof of my mouth. Ah! I start to suck really hard, as if I'm milking him. He comes in a thick, frothy spray, which I swallow willingly. Strange, how I adore my own sense of complete and utter submission to this man. I wriggle my hips.

'Don't you dare move,' he warns.

I don't. Very gently, I keep sucking the semi-hard flesh in my mouth. I work on it until it starts to stretch and grow and become rock hard. I take his cock out of my mouth,

and, crawling down his body, poise my pussy over his erection.

'I want to hear the animal noises you make,' he says.

I hold onto the base of his shaft while he groans with pleasure as his erect cock slowly fills me up. Once all of him is inside me, I ride him with rhythmic, languid thrusts, and animal sounds fill the bedroom until we come, gripping each other so hard he leaves marks on my skin.

'I don't want to sleep the whole night,' he whispers fiercely.

'Why?' I whisper back.

'Just this one night I don't want to close my eyes. All I want to do is make— Fuck all night.'

'OK,' I say, but we do fall asleep. Curled up against each other like two puppies in a basket. And we sleep soundly until the wee hours of the morning when a large hand crashes into my ribs and shocks me awake.

I sit up and see Dom thrashing his legs and moving his hands restlessly.

I switch on my bedside lamp and start shaking him and urgently calling his name. His eyes fly open. They are wild with horror. They fasten on me and widen with shock.

He rises off the pillows and grabs my upper arms, but I have the impression that I've become part of the nightmare that he's still locked into. 'I thought you were dead,' he says in a strange voice.

'I'm not,' I say.

 184

At the sound of my voice he suddenly lets go of my arms. He falls back on the pillows and covers his eyes with his forearm.

'Oh! God!' he howls. The sound comes from somewhere so deep and pained that I become frozen with fear.

A few seconds pass before I shuffle closer. 'Tell me, please, Dom. Just tell me what's wrong?' I beg.

He puts his arm down and looks at me. 'You're a good person, Ella. But I just can't do this anymore. It's a lie. All of it is a lie.'

He vaults off the bed and begins to dress.

'You're going to leave now?' I ask in disbelief.

'I'm sorry,' he says, and, without looking at me, walks out of my door.

I sit there stunned. I have no idea what the hell has just happened. Has he just fucking broken up with me?

Bang, bang, my baby shot me down!

TWENTY

Ella

I stand at the window in a daze and listen to his car come to life with such an explosive sound that it makes me jump. I don't go back to bed after he speeds off. Maybe because I cannot believe that he will not come back.

We were going so good. It seems incredible that he would raze the city and salt the earth just like that. Over nothing. Nothing earth-shattering has happened. I stepped onto the road without looking, but it wasn't like I was in any real danger. It would be a stretch of the imagination to even think so.

It doesn't make sense. Nothing makes sense.

Unless it is in some way connected to that terrible grief that lives deep inside him. The one I accidentally glimpsed when I went back into the restaurant for Rob's umbrella that first day. When I found him so curled up with pain that he reminded me of a wounded beast. The kind of suffering that is so blind and raw that approach is dangerous and any attempt to help would be suicidal.

I pace the flat incessantly, stopping only to throw a double vodka down my throat. I find myself back at the window looking down at the deserted street, as if in disbelief. We've never spent a night apart ever since the first night I spent at his house. After two hours of waiting, I finally admit to myself that he's not coming back. Not tonight, anyway.

I go and sit dry-eyed in front of the television. I recognize that I'm watching a movie, but beyond that I don't register anything. All I can see before my eyes is the moment he ripped my chest open with a knife by saying, 'I just can't do this anymore.'

Do what? I haven't pushed or tried to get from him anything that he didn't want to give. I switch off the TV and put on my CD player. Whitney Houston's 'I Will Always Love You' comes on. It grates on my nerves. I switch it off with a grunt. The flat becomes horribly silent.

I rush to fill it with sound. I pick Vangelis. It's Dom's favorite. Beautiful, dramatic music fills the air, but for some reason the only thing I want to listen to is 'Stairway to Heaven'. The wistful longing and mysterious lyrics suit my mood. I listen to Heart's rendition of the song.

In my condition it seems to me that the arrangement of music is in timeless layers that open up like a flower to reveal a yearning, fragile soul calling for something almost forgotten.

When Heart's version ends, I move on to Dolly Parton's. As soon as I've listened to her, I put on Led Zepplin's original version. Then I go back to Heart's version. Obsessively, I open my laptop and look at street performers singing the song. Again and again I return to Heart's version. I listen and I listen. As if the solution to my problem is hidden in the song.

But there is no solution.

I am the woman who thought that everything that glitters is gold. The one who was building a stairway to heaven, but, as Dom once told me, my stairway is whispering in the wind.

When dawn breaks in the sky I am still listening to music.

Dom doesn't call even in the morning.

I go to work, a wreck. I open the door to my office and look at my desk with dread. I hate this temporary job I took last week where I have to field on-line complaints all day about packages that have not arrived, are delayed, lost, or damaged. My job is to calmly absorb their frustration and send them on the relevant department.

The dreary drudgery of it has to be seen to be believed. At least when I was at HMRC I felt I was doing something good. There was always that feeling that I counted for something.

Here, I'm a cog in the wheel.

I truly count for nothing. Perhaps I should have listened to Dom. Perhaps I should have taken his offer of money and waited until I found a better job. But I couldn't bring myself to do that. I was too proud. And now I think, Thank God I didn't take his money.

No matter how bad this job is, at least it pays my bills.

I sit at my desk and jump every time my phone rings. Sometimes I stare at it as if I can metaphysically make him call me. I wait and wait. Until lunchtime, until I can bear it no more. I pick up my phone and call Jake.

'Hey, Ella,' he says. His tone is surprised and cautious.

'Hello, Jake. I ... uh ... Can I talk to you ... um ... alone?'

'Of course,' he says immediately, and his tone tells me what I suspected. He knows exactly what's wrong with Dom.

'Thank you, Jake.'

'No problem. We're in the country tonight. Want to come over for dinner? I can send a car.'

'No, no. No need for that, I'll borrow a friend's car. And I won't disturb you at dinnertime. I'll come just before that.'

'All right, see you about six thirty.'

'That'll be great. Thank you.'

'You know how to get to mine, right?'

'Yes. I'll see you then.'

'See you later.'

'Jake?'

'Yeah?'

'I really appreciate this.'

I hear him draw in a sharp breath. 'That's OK, Ella. I'm always happy to help.'

I park Anna's company car next to Lily's Mercedes-Benz and walk up to the front door. Smoothing down my hair, I ring on the doorbell. Lily opens the door with a smile.

'Hello,' she greets.

'Hey,' I say awkwardly.

She opens the door wider. 'Come on in,' she invites.

I step into her home. Lily is one of those women who have it all. Happiness, beauty, love, wealth.

She's wearing a long, halter-neck dress that comes to her ankles. It's one of those dresses that you know cost an arm and a leg. Once, a dress like that would have sent me to my computer to see if her husband's tax records matched that level of expenditure, but those days are gone. It feels as if the notion that I was a tax officer at Her

Majesty's Revenue Customs was another life, or just a dream of mine.

I smile at her. 'Congratulations. I heard you're pregnant.'

She rubs her belly and smiles contentedly. 'Yes, thank you, Ella. And how have you been keeping?'

'Good,' I say.

'Jake's expecting you. He's in his den. Do you want to come through and have a drink before you see him?'

'No. No, thank you,' I refuse politely.

Liliana runs in from one of the reception rooms, screaming, 'Aunty Ella, Aunty Ella.'

She is wearing a pink skirt and a T-shirt that states in bold letters 'My Mother Thinks She's The Boss'. I go down on my haunches. 'My, my, look how much you've grown since I last saw you.'

'That was yesterday,' she says scornfully.

'Dear me. Yes, that was yesterday.'

'My poo was blue today,' she declares suddenly.

'Oh,' I exclaim.

'Lil,' her mother reprimands, 'what did I tell you about telling the whole world about the color of your poo?'

'Aunty Ella is not the whole world,' Liliana argues with impeccable logic. She turns her adorable face toward me. 'My poo was made of icing.'

I straighten and look at Lily.

'She went to a birthday party yesterday and ate too much blue icing from a Thomas the Tank Engine cake,' Lily explains

Even though I was distraught, it made me giggle. How utterly sweet.

'Where's Uncle Dom?' Liliana demands.

The laughter dies in my throat. 'I ... I have no idea.' Voicing the thought saddens me greatly. Far more than I would have expected.

'Lil, Aunty Ella has come to see Daddy. Say bye-bye now.' She looks at me with an encouraging smile. 'Go on, Ella. It's just at the end of the corridor.'

'See you later, Liliana,' I call as I start walking down it.

'Can I go and sit with Daddy and Aunty Ella?' I hear Liliana ask her mother plaintively.

'No, you can't.'

'Why not?' the minx demands.

I don't hear Lily's answer because I'm already too far away, or they've moved into one of the other rooms. It hits me then: I'm not part of this family, and it looks like I never will be. I stand for a moment outside the door at the end of the corridor. Taking a deep breath, I knock.

It is opened almost immediately.

'Come in,' Jake invites cordially.

He is wearing a black T-shirt and gray jeans, and I must admit, just being in his presence makes me nervous. He is as big and intimidating as Dom, but there are absolutely no buttons to push. No weakness. No secret sadness to exploit. He is one of those smoothly impenetrable and guarded people. It was always clear to me that he is the boss of his family. He guards them as ferociously as a mother lion guards her newborn babies.

Woe betide *anyone* who tries to hurt them.

'Thanks,' I say quietly, and step into a large, wood-paneled room. It has soft rugs, a heavy wooden desk at one end of the room, and a nest of expensive leather couches at the other end. There is an air of old world opulence about it all. Here, one can feel safe and cultured. The outside world never intrudes. Here, Jake is King. From here, he controls his empire.

He gestures toward the sofas.

I move over to them. My legs feel like jelly and my skin is tingling with nervous energy. Stop it, I tell myself. *You have nothing to fear.* I am on the same side as Jake. I don't want to hurt Dom. I love him. It is perfectly obvious that he is in terrible pain, and I just want to help him.

'I was just about to have a drink. Would you like to join me?' he says.

I start to shake my head and then decide that I actually do need something strong to calm me. 'I'll have whatever you're having.'

'I'm having a whiskey,' he says, and I nod.

He moves toward a drinks trolley. With his back to me he pours two fingers of whiskey into two glasses and comes toward me. As he crosses the room, he passes the last rays of evening light coming from the window. They hit the side of his face and I am struck by how handsome all the Eden brothers are.

I take the glass and bring it to my lips. The whiskey is strong and hits my empty stomach like liquid fire.

Jake doesn't say anything, simply watches me with a deliberately bland expression. I know that his first and most natural instinct is to protect his brother. These gypsies stick together. For them, blood will always be thicker than water. He will help me, but only if it means it will also benefit his brother.

Fuck it. I decide to take the bull by the horns.

'Last night Dom had a nightmare. When I woke him up he thought I was dead. And then he... he ... said he couldn't continue our relationship anymore and walked out of my flat. I haven't spoken to or seen him since. Can you tell me anything that would help me understand what's going on, Jake? I ... I'm ... really ... um ... in love with your brother.'

An expression of pity crosses his face. He takes a gulp of whiskey and turns his face away from mine. Seconds pass in silence. He appears to be looking into a distant past. At something that saddens him very much.

He turns to me. 'When Dom was seventeen years old, he fell in love with a girl. She was sixteen. A laughing, wild, rebellious gypsy girl. Her name was Vivien. He thought they were soul mates because they were both so crazy and so alike. They could finish each other's sentences. He wanted to marry her straightaway, but I forced him to wait until he was eighteen.

'"You have your whole life ahead of you. What's the hurry?" I told him. The truth was, I disapproved of her. She was bad for him. Too wild. She took too many risks. She egged him on, dared him to new and dangerous adventures. The kind of things that could land him in prison. Together, they reminded me of Bonnie and Clyde. I hoped, I prayed it would not last.

'But I was wrong. The love he had for her didn't die. It just became stronger. They became inseparable. After his eighteenth birthday, very reluctantly, I started to make plans. Everything was ready. In one month they would have been married, but then she did something no one had ever dreamed she would. I don't know how she did it, but she stowed away on a smugglers' boat that Dom was on.

'It was night and the sea was rough. Something happened on that boat. She fell overboard and was swept away.'

TWENTY-ONE

Dom

With the swiftness of a gull, Vivien went over. She rushed to her fate, so near to me that I know I could have caught her if only I'd put my hand out.

Her hopeless, terror-stricken, doomed face, I saw for merely a moment, but it would be forever etched in my soul. The wide, laughing mouth had become a dark hole in her white face, and her beautiful, dancing eyes were huge with shock. Legs wheeling. Arms flailing. Desperate .... Oh God! How desperately she had looked for something to hold on to, anything, other than salty, gray air and diagonally flashing rain.

The cast iron rule was:
If you fall overboard that's your fucking funeral. *The boat stops for NOTHING.*

One look at Preston and Dallas and I knew: they had absolutely no intention of

stopping. Hardly surprising since the pair were certifiable psychopaths. It was the reason Jake wouldn't have anything to do with them. But me, I had to be the big I AM. I had to work with the most dangerous thugs in Britain to prove what a tough guy I was.

So ...

They wouldn't stop. I couldn't overpower them—both carried guns. The choice was simple to make. I didn't think. I didn't hesitate. Not for one second. In a flash I pulled out a lifejacket from under the canopy and, with it clutched in my hand, I vaulted over the side of the vessel into the roiling sea, as far away from the pull of the boat as possible.

I hit the water, and sank quickly into a pitch-black abyss full of bubbles. Using my arms to counteract the downward pull, I fought and kicked my way back up, and burst onto the surface with a great gasp. I knew when I jumped overboard that the sea was choppy and treacherous, but in the light of a three-quarter moon it looked as if I was in the middle of a mass of boiling black oil.

Fortunately, it was late July and, though the water was cold, it wasn't paralyzing. At a guess I would say it was just over fifty degrees Fahrenheit. In that temperature a man could survive for a good few hours before hypothermia set in. That is, if he was wearing a lifejacket or had something to hold on to.

I was wearing my GPS tracker, and I knew that either Preston or Dallas would radio Jake to let him know what had happened, and he would come for me. But it could be hours. I could survive, but what about Vivien? She was small, and the shock of falling into the water would have caused her to swallow a lot of salt water. I looked around frantically.

Until you've been alone in the middle of an endless stretch of water, you don't know how truly small and insignificant you are. I was like cork bobbing on an unforgiving, restless landscape that contained absolutely nothing, not one fucking thing. It had swallowed everything.

She was nowhere to be seen.

I screamed for her over the sound of the boat's engine, but there was no reply. Telling myself that she wasn't scared of water, she was a good swimmer, and she was young with a robust constitution, I hooked my hand through one of the armholes of the lifejacket and began to swim strongly toward the area where she'd fallen.

But the truth was I was petrified. I'd never been more afraid in my life. My body was pumping with adrenalin. The raw panic surging through me was tempered only by incredulity that *this* was actually happening to *me*.

In my head my father was saying, *Don't thrash about, lad. Keep still. Float. And don't fuckin' stretch your hand out—it cools the body. Use your legs. Conserve your heat. Conserve your heat. Conserve your heat ...* But my hands and legs were moving about wildly. There was no thought of conserving heat.

The sound of the boat died away and I stopped swimming. Treading water, I shouted out to her, and listened. Nothing. *Where the fuck is she?* My heart was beating so hard I felt it bang in my ears. I knew if I didn't get to her soon, she would die.

I turned round and round, scanning the dark, restless water, hoping, praying. And then, with a surge of excitement, I saw her. She had just colored her hair—the most horrendous orange you ever saw—and I hated it, but it was glowing and floating like seaweed in the moonlight.

Jesus!

She was floating face down! Like a doll being tossed about in the waves.

Fuck me, Vivien! You were planning to go down without a word.

Kicking quickly and powerfully, I swam up to her and threw my arm in a bear hug across her lifeless body. It frightened me how totally unaware of me she was. Grabbing her biceps, I spun her around so she was facing upwards. Still holding on to her body, I swam under her and emerged on the other side of her head, so her back was lying on my chest.

Her eyes were closed, her skin was cold and bluish, and her head lolled. I squeezed her with both forearms in the way you would

if someone had swallowed something that was blocking their airways. To my horror, I had crushed her so hard I heard a crack. I prayed I had not broken a rib. *A broken rib won't matter if she's dead*, a voice in my head said.

I was suddenly engulfed by the most horrendous fear.

I don't know how I did it with the waves bashing us on all sides, and the plumes of spray that hit us in the face, but I managed to grab her tight, pinch her nose with my other hand, and blow into her mouth while pressing the heel of my hand on her diaphragm thirty times, twice a second. I kept on doing it until she coughed, vomited a load of salt water out, and started gulping summer air.

I felt a surge of fierce joy. Quickly inflating the lifejacket, I began to massage her shivering body, keeping her skin as close to mine as possible. She came back to life slowly. The first thing she did was fucking apologize.

It made me so angry. 'Shut up, Vivien. Don't you dare apologize. We said we'd never say sorry to each other. We're the wild ones, remember?'

'I can't believe we're going to end up as shark food,' she said. There was no fear in her voice. Maybe she was in shock.

'These waters are too cold for sharks,' I replied, rubbing her arms furiously. I knew we were a long way from being saved.

 201

'So this is how my life ends,' she said in a voice full of wonder.

It hit me in the chest like a kick from a horse. 'You're not fucking dying. Stop being so fucking dramatic.'

She turned her head slightly and looked at me sadly. 'I feel so stupid. This is the stupidest thing I've done. I can't believe I'm going to die because of my own stupidity,' she whispered. And then the thought occurred to her. 'Oh my God, Dom. I've been so selfish. You're going to die too.'

'Neither of us is going to die. Jake will be here soon.'

'What if he doesn't come? He doesn't like me, you know,' she said.

'Stop talking nonsense. Why wouldn't he like you?'

'You're such a fool, Dom.'

'He'll come.'

'What if he doesn't make it in time?'

'He'll make it in time,' I said, a wave slapping salt water into my mouth.

'I'm sorry, baby.'

I could feel the rage in my guts. 'Stop apologizing. I'd do the same again given half the chance.'

'If I die, will you marry someone else?'

'I'll never marry anyone else, Vivien.'

'I couldn't bear it if you do.'

'Look, I fucking won't, OK?'

'You promise?'

'I promise.'

'I'll come back and haunt you if you do.'

'You're not going to fucking die, so this is a stupid discussion.'

'But if I do. Don't fall in love with anyone else.'

'You won't,' I said through clenched teeth.

She didn't speak anymore, and for more than an hour both of us were mostly silent. We spoke only to check that we were both still alive. I kept glancing at my watch every few minutes. Time had never moved so slowly. After what seemed like interminable hours my legs felt like dead weights and I was struggling to move them.

By then, Vivien was also no longer shivering. There was a strange lethargy about her. I knew that at that rate she was not going to last. I turned her over so her chest was pressed to mine. It was harder work for me, but I didn't know what else to do to warm her up.

'Don't move unless you have to. Don't even kick your legs. Stay still and conserve your energy,' I told her.

'I'm afraid, Dom. I'm afraid I'll die.' Her voice was quivering with emotion.

'No, you fucking won't. I won't allow it.'

'My wedding dress. You'll never see me in my wedding dress,' she moaned into my neck.

The dank taste of the ocean was in my mouth. 'I'll fucking see you in your wedding dress if I have to bury you in it,' I growled.

She giggled. It was a weak, lazy sound. She was slipping away. I could feel it as strongly as I knew my hands had become so numb I could no longer feel them.

'It doesn't hurt like I thought it would. I'm not scared anymore. It's almost peaceful, actually. Just like falling into something soft and dark.'

I held her tighter still. 'Vivien, you have to fight it. Stay with me.'

'Hey, baby! Look at those lights. They're beauuuuuuutiful.'

'What lights?'

'Can you not see them?'

'No.'

'Oh, I pity you. They are sooooo beautiful.'

I gazed down at her face. It was animated in a way it had not been since I'd found her floating face down. I became terrified.

'Vivien, look at me,' I shouted, but she was so entranced by the vision in front of her that she refused to turn in my direction. I grabbed her chin and turned her face toward me. Her eyes were glassy and empty. They seemed unable to focus on me. She made a small, incoherent sound of displeasure or irritation.

'The lights. I want to see the lights,' she mumbled pleadingly.

I released her chin and she turned away immediately to gaze with fascination at the lights only she could see. I looked around desperately at the empty blackness stretching out in all directions around us. And I prayed. And I prayed.

It felt like we had been in the water forever.

My legs were getting tired of treading water, and I could see that she had given up the desire to fight the cold. Not even the lights could interest her anymore. Her eyes were closing. Her body, having imposed increasingly drastic measures to keep functioning, was finally starting to shut down. Her heartbeat was becoming weaker and weaker. If I didn't do something soon it would stop completely. Then only her brain would be alive. And then even that would die. I *had* to pull her out of her slump.

I shook her and she opened her eyes weakly.

'Listen,' I said with fake excitement. 'Jake's coming. I can hear the engine of his boat.'

She seemed to listen. 'I don't hear it,' she mumbled groggily.

'There's too much water in your ears,' I lied.

She smiled weakly, only half-conscious. 'I'm so happy. He can take me back to my mother,' she said, and I smiled back, but my smile became a grimace of horror when her heart stopped and she died from the sheer relief of thinking that she had been rescued.

I couldn't believe it.

I'd heard of people dying from the relief of thinking they'd been rescued, but I had never thought that it would happen to her. I held her body tightly against mine. It was impossible that she was gone. I couldn't comprehend that something as alive as she could ever succumb to something as ordinary as death. Or that as fierce and possessive as my love was, I couldn't keep her. I had held on so tightly, with every ounce of my being, and yet she had slipped away, like sand from a clenched fist.

So I shook her limp body. I rubbed her arms and legs. I gave her mouth-to-mouth resuscitation, but Vivien was gone. The pain and horror of losing her was unbearable. Words couldn't enter into my pain. I began to scream. I screamed and screamed like a madman. I cursed, I swore, I sobbed until no sounds would come out of my mouth.

I kissed her cold, blue lips.

'Oh, Vivien!'

In my head she was wearing a red rose in her hair and whispering, 'You're my gypsy hero. You'll always be my gypsy hero.'

'Oh, Vivien!'

Once there was a way to get back home
again...
___
https://www.youtube.com/watch?v=LjOl0fG72ZE

TWENTY-TWO

Ella

'When we pulled their waterlogged bodies out of the water, Dom was nearly as blue as Vivien. He never uttered a single sound, not pain, not grief, not relief. His fingers were so tightly clenched around her corpse it was ages before we could prize them away from her cold flesh. He stared vacantly into the distance. When I called him, he turned slowly and looked at me as if he didn't recognize me. As if we were not flesh and blood.'

Jake stops speaking, and I see him shudder with the terrible memory.

'I brought him to my house and put him in my bed. He slept for three hours. Then came the profuse diarrhea brought on by the seawater he'd ingested, and the uncontrollable muscle tremors. He became very ill, and Shane and I took care of him. He even missed her funeral. They buried her in her wedding dress, apparently in accordance with her wishes. She had told her mother that if she should die before her wedding she was to be buried in her dress.'

As Jake speaks, a numbing cold is creeping into my body, and I hug myself and force myself to listen to his words.

'Dom was so ill that for a while we even thought he was going to die. But he didn't. His body grew stronger, even if his head was totally fucked. For weeks he had such severe nightmares that he would move bedroom furniture around in his sleep and wake up screaming on the floor. He was like a madman. He blamed himself. He couldn't look at a picture of her without getting into an uncontrollable rage. I gathered up all the photos of her and hid them.

'Then one day I came back and he was making himself an omelet. "Want one?" he asked, and I knew it was going to be all right. We ate together and he thanked me for everything I'd done. Then he left.'

Jake looks at me with somber, sad eyes. 'Ever since then there has been no other woman in his life. One-night stands, casual flings. No woman, no matter how hard they tried, and believe me when I tell you a lot tried, and very hard too, could get close to him. Until you.'

Jake pauses and takes a sip of whiskey while watching me intently from above the rim of his glass.

I drop my eyes. Some part of me feels a flash of joy at his last sentence, but it's muted. I think I'm in shock.

'Don't give up on him so quickly. He's come so far because of you,' Jake says, as if he's trying to sell me the idea of staying in a relationship with Dom. As if he needs to.

I look up at him suddenly and his eyes slide away. Not immediately, but he can't hold my gaze! I watch him take another sip before he raises his eyes to me. I stare at him. He looks back without flinching this time, but that moment he couldn't hold my gaze has given him away.

'There's more, isn't there?' I ask.

He sighs. It's actually a sound of relief. As if a burden is about to be lifted from his shoulders.

He nods, stands, and walks over to his desk. He unlocks the last drawer and takes a photo album out. He turns the pages to somewhere in the middle and walks back to me carrying the open album. He stands over me and holds the book out to me.

I take it from him. It's one of those fancy albums with tracing paper between the pages holding the photos. I take the end of the tracing paper page and turn it, and pretty much just stare at the picture. It's a photo taken outside some kind of temple. The sun is shining brightly. I'm wearing a pink tie-dyed T-shirt and a long flowery skirt. It looks like it's been taken in a foreign land. India, perhaps. Asia, definitely.

But I've never been to Asia.

All these impressions hit me in seconds. I raise my eyes upwards and Jake is looking down at me, his eyes full of pity.

'That's her?' I ask in a shocked whisper.

'That's Vivien.'

'Oh my God!' I cry. The girl in the photo looks exactly like me. The similarity is uncanny. Except for her hair color, I am her twin.

'I'm sorry,' Jake says softly.

Suddenly *everything* makes sense. Everything! It explains why the whole family had behaved so strangely when Dom introduced me. I'd thought it was because Dom was dating a tax inspector, but now I know. Ah! That would nicely explain away the uneasy, quickly hidden expression on his mother's face whenever she thought I wasn't looking.

A thought seeds itself into my head.

'Did you already know what I looked like when we met?'

'Yes, Shane had warned us all.'

I nod slowly, taking the information in. 'Did Shane know Vivien?'

He frowns. 'Of course. Dom was going to marry her.'

'I see.' Some part of my rational brain makes the observation that only Shane in this family is truly impenetrable. His classically handsome face had betrayed nothing when he had met me for the first time at the party.

Nothing but an open friendliness and an irresistible charm.

'Right,' I say slowly. My whole life is falling apart around me. 'So, Dom went out with me because I reminded him of his dead fiancée.'

'I'm sure the fact that you look like her has something to do with it, but you're totally different in every way.'

I look at him with disbelieving eyes.

'Everything about you is different. She was selfish, tempestuous, controlling and impulsive, and you are careful, kind, considerate and deep.'

Oh my God. The way he describes me makes me sound so boring. I cover my eyes with the palms of my hands. What a fucking mess!

Jake comes over and goes down on his haunches in front of me. Startled, I uncover my eyes. Jake at close quarters is an intimidating experience. It's like being too close to a live wire. Part of me wants to move away.

As if he knows that I am uncomfortable, he fixes me with his mesmerizing eyes and moves in for the kill. 'Remember, when I said Vivien was no good for him, I truly meant it. You are the perfect match. You balance him and bring out the best in him. You make him happy.'

'But he wants her. She is his true soul mate. I'm just a poor imitation.' It hurts like hell to voice the thought. I feel the tears start welling up in my eyes.

'Ella, listen to me. He was eighteen. She was his first love. Do you remember what you were like when you were eighteen? If he had married her, it would have been a disaster, and they would have ended up hating each other and getting divorced. But because she died, she has become his dancing queen, young and sweet, only seventeen. A great, lost love. But he has suffered enough. She's gone, and you're here.'

'I'm nothing to him.'

'You have no idea what you've done for him. The demons had completely taken over when you came into his life. You broke them up with your softness.'

I stare at him wordlessly. How much I want to believe him, but my heart feels like it's breaking into pieces. He never wanted me. He was trying to replace her. When he was touching me, he was really touching her.

'He never really wanted me,' I sob. 'The whole time he was pretending I was her.'

He reaches out a hand and touches my cheek. His hand is warm and gentle. And it makes me want to lean into it for the comfort it holds.

'Ah, Ella. You're not a man. I am. Take it from me. My brother wanted Vivien the way a boy wants a girl. He wants you with the passion with which a man wants a woman. Let him discover that. Give him a chance.

There's a lot of Dom that you've not seen yet.'
He smiles tenderly and removes his hand.

I stare at him through a film of tears. The kindness and softness that he's showing has surprised me. He always looks so unreachable and aloof.

'But he doesn't want to be with me anymore,' I say softly.

'If you believed that you wouldn't be here now.'

I sniff. 'So what do I do? Wait for him to come to me?'

He shrugs. 'I won't tell you what to do, but if I were you I wouldn't let anything stand in the way of something I wanted. I'd go and fight for it until it was mine or I had died trying. The journey has just begun and the destination could be a very beautiful place.'

He stands, and walks away from me toward his desk. He comes back with a box of tissues. I pull out a couple and wipe my face. Then I stand.

'I should be going,' I say.

'I'll walk you to your car.'

'There's no need.'

'I want to,' he says with a gentle smile.

I turn toward him. 'Thank you, Jake.'

'I'll always be here for you. Don't give your ear to the devil.'

To love too much is to lick honey from the point of a knife.

TWENTY-THREE

I think I was OK while I was in Jake's house. While I was saying goodbye to Lily and Liliana. I was even OK when Jake closed the car door for me and waved me away.

It hits me when I'm on the motorway.

Suddenly my windpipe feels like it is full of concrete. I can't breathe. I swerve into the hard shoulder. Horns blare. I screech to a stop. I feel as if I'm suffocating. I open the car door and stumble out. I lurch to the edge of the road and collapse holding my throat. I take shallow breaths.

On my hands and knees, I pant until I feel my airways open. Cars whoosh past at great speed. Somebody thinks to stop his car up ahead. A man runs toward me. I hold my hand up, the palm facing him to tell him not to come forward. He stops a few yards away.

'Are you OK?'

I nod.

'Do you want me to call an ambulance?'

I shake my head.

'You sure?'

I nod and smile weakly at him.

'Want me to wait with you?'

I shake my head again, touched by the kindness of this stranger.

He raises his hand in some kind of acknowledgment and, turning around, starts to walk away.

'Hey,' I call out.

He turns back.

'Thank you.'

'It's all right,' he says, and with a backward wave returns to his car. I watch him drive away. I sit by the side of the road, and, with the engine of my car still running, I burst into a flood of tears. When it's all over, I get back into my car and drive home. There, I stand in the shower and let the water wash away my pain. I wrap myself in a robe and call Anna. I tell her everything.

'I'm coming over,' she says. 'Put some shot glasses in the freezer.'

'Oh, Anna,' I sigh, tears filling my eyes.

'We need to get drunk. It's been ages.'

She arrives at my doorstep with two bottles of her father's homemade gooseberry vodka. She gets the cold glasses out of the freezer and pours us a shot each. The sweet, sharp taste is like summer in a glass.

I down another shot and put the glass on the coffee table with a thump. One bottle is rolling on the floor and this bottle is almost half empty.

Anna claps her hands excitedly. 'I know what. You should become the coffee beans,' she slurs.

I frown blearily. 'The coffee beans?'

'You know. From the story on the Internet about the grandmother, the broccoli.' She stops, her eyes narrowed. 'No, wait. It wasn't broccoli. It was carrots. Yeah, that's right, the carrots, the eggs and the coffee beans.'

'I don't know the story.'

She sits straighter. 'This woman gets cheated on—'

'That's not my situation,' I protest immediately.

She waves her hand airily. 'Just wait for the end, will ya?'

'Go on.'

'She goes to her grandmother and asks for her advice. The grandmother puts three pots of water on the stove. Into one pot she puts broccoli.'

'Carrots,' I correct.

She nods sagely. 'I was just checking to see if you were listening.'

'Yeah, right.'

'Now that we've established that you're paying attention, we'll carry on. And in the other two pots she puts the other two ingredients.'

 218

'Eggs and coffee beans.'

'Exactly.'

I sigh. Even though I am so drunk, I can't get Dom out of my head.

'She lets all the ingredients boil for twenty minutes.'

'Why twenty minutes?'

'Do you want to hear this story or not?'

'Go on,' I say, and reach for the bottle again.

'She takes all the ingredients out, and basically shows her granddaughter that the carrots went in strong and hard and came out soft and malleable. The eggs went in soft and came out hardened. Only the coffee beans elevated themselves to another level, released their fragrance and flavor, and changed the water. So all three objects faced the same suffering and adversity, but each reacted differently. When the situation gets hot, you have to decide which are you.'

I put the bottle down. 'I feel like the carrots at the moment.'

'That's today. What will you be tomorrow and the day after?'

I drop my forehead into my palm. 'Oh, Anna. My life is such a mess. I thought I was in such a good place—and now look at me! My world was like a bubble waiting to pop.'

'Hey, look on the bright side. At least she's dead.'

'What?' I gasp.

'Yeah. At least she's not around to disturb your fragile peace of mind with cruel physical comparisons.'

'What do you mean?'

'I mean I have a raging aversion to *all* my boyfriend's exes. Like, seriously detest, abhor, and hate them. I get so jealous that I can't stop pouring over their Facebook photos to examine their tans, their smiles, their outfits, in the hope of finding faults so that later I can subtly criticize them while in conversation with my boyfriend.'

She stops and picks at her nail polish.

'In fact, one or two I've hated so much I even fantasized about breaking into their houses and stabbing them while they slept in their beds.'

'Really?' I ask, shocked.

'Absolutely. It's petty and childish, but I can't help it. It's like an addiction because I'm so insecure. I feel as if I'm in competition with them. I'd much rather a dead girlfriend who looks like me.'

'No, I'd rather have an ex who's alive. I can't even consider pouring over her Facebook pictures to subtly criticize her because she's been put on some kind of pedestal. I mean how do you compete against a dead woman?' I ask garrulously.

'God! I hate exes. Alive or dead, they're just trouble. Talking about exes, I forgot to ask before, have you heard from your stalker?'

I shrug. 'I think I frightened him off.'

'No more midnight phone calls?'

'No more,' I mumble. The room has started to spin. 'I need to pee and to get to bed,' I say, and stand up unsteadily.

She stands and we use the bathroom together. Then she helps me to bed.

'Sleep next to me,' I tell her.

She smiles down at me. There's a strange, pitying look on her face as she stands over me.

TWENTY-FOUR

I, stalker

I stand over her and a thrill runs through me.

I am in her space, her bedroom! How strange that hatred, in its intensity and viscosity, should be so similar to passion. Look at her! Sleeping the gentle sleep of angels. So beautiful. So innocent. Bitch!

I take a step closer. My shoes are soft-soled and make no sound. It is a warm night and a window is open. Gentle breezes make the curtains flutter. Otherwise, everything is perfectly still. It is dark, but my eyes are accustomed to the dark. I have embraced the dark, made it my friend, taken it and its terrible secrets into my heart.

I bend down so that I am only a few inches from her skin.

How sweet and divine she smells. And yet, she destroyed me without a second thought. I still remember the first time I saw her waltzing across a room and thought, wow! She's hot. I didn't know she was a half-woman, half-serpent. But I was a man then.

She changed me, made me into the thing I am now, a shell. I loved her for so long. But there is nothing in my life now except this all-consuming obsession I have for her. Look at her throat. The seductive curve begs you to kiss it, wrap your fingers possessively around it, and squeeze it, until her eyes fly open and watch you in horror even as her pussy curls helplessly around your rock-hard dick.

Very gently, I blow into her slightly parted lips. My stale vapors enter her pink mouth. I will contaminate you yet further, my sweet.

'Mmm...' she murmurs.

I freeze.

She moves away from my warm breath. Even in sleep she is moving away from me. I guess she only wants a big man. I have seen her with him. He holds her possessively. He would make a formidable enemy, but I will not be confronting him. I will just be taking her away from him.

Why? Because she is mine.

Let him be broken, the way I was, when he took her away from me. I've taken care of all the other men who have sniffed around her like wild animals. It was easy because she didn't want them. She wants this one. I have followed her up to his house in the woods, which he never locks, and watched from the

window as he fucked her. It made me sick to my stomach. I threw up in the bushes. I thought she was something special.

Cheap hussy was mewling like a kitten for his dick.

I feel my cock harden. So. My body still wants the little bitch. I shall have her. I shall tie her up and have her until my body feels the disgust and abhorrence my mind feels for her. I would take her today, if not for the other woman sleeping in her bed. My opportunity will come again. One of these days she will be alone again. And I will strike then.

I straighten, and, turning my head, look at my own visage. How curious. It is a pale and glowing mask in the moonlight. Looking back at me is the almost demonic face of a man possessed by rage and hatred.

Vengeance will be mine.

I stand there for a long time. Only when I have had my fill of my complete power over her vulnerable form do I turn around and leave the way I had come.

Through the front door.

TWENTY-FIVE

Dom

The wound is the place where the light enters
you.

—Rumi

I knock at the semi-detached house and Vivien's mother opens the door. The past ten years have not been kind to her.

'Hello, Mirela.'

'Hello, Dom,' she says with a smile, and moves back to let me in.

I go into the living room and look around me. Nothing seems to have changed. Everything is spotless. The kitsch decorations, the fans on the walls, the patterned carpet, the net curtains, the ornate figurines, and the bohemian crystal vases filled with plastic flowers. She gestures for me to sit.

I sit on an armchair with a crocheted lace antimacassar. The cushion is old and

lumpy. I feel a sense of guilt. I should have come earlier. I should have given them some financial help. I know Jake gave money, but I should have done something too.

She takes a seat opposite me. There is a low coffee table with an oval lacy doily-like thing between us. On it she has set a crystal bowl filled with sugared almonds, a tray with a teapot and cups, and a plate covered with a napkin. She smiles at me mistily and begins pouring the tea. She doesn't ask how I like my tea. She pours exactly the right amount of milk and drops in a cube of sugar. She hands it over to me.

'Thank you,' I say, accepting the dainty china.

She lifts the napkin off the plate and reveals thinly sliced rectangles of marble cake. She picks up the plate and holds it out to me. 'Your favorite,' she says.

Something heavy lodges in my heart. I've been so selfish. I take a slice and hold it awkwardly in my fingers

'How have you been?' she asks, pouring herself a cup of tea.

'I've been all right.'

She looks up. 'I'm so glad to hear that. I've been waiting for you to come for ten years.'

My eyes widen with shock. 'Why?'

'I knew you'd come when the pain was gone.'

I draw a sharp breath. 'The pain is not gone.'

She half smiles. 'I'm sorry. Of course. The pain never goes. But it lessens. That's what I meant to say. When the pain lessened.' She drops a couple of cubes of sugar into her tea and stirs it with a teaspoon. I watch her lift it to her lips and sip at it delicately. She puts the cup and saucer back on the coffee table.

'Eat, eat,' she encourages.

I bite into the slice of cake. The smell and taste of it roll the years back. It is as if I am eighteen again. It is an old ritual, the two of us having tea and cake while I wait for Vivien to come out of her bedroom, all dolled up, and ready to paint the town red. I gaze into her eyes and wonder if she has traveled back with me, but she hasn't. She doesn't need to. She is still trapped there. She has not moved on. Everything in this house is exactly like it was when I was last here a decade ago. In this world of lace and plastic flowers, I could maybe turn my head toward the corridor and maybe, just maybe Vivien will walk through.

The knowledge is like a flash of lightning that lights up a black sky with white light. Vivien is not Ella. They are as different as oranges and oysters. Only in appearance are they alike. In temperament and personality no two women could be more unlike than Vivien and Ella. And that streak of lightning makes something else crystal clear.

I'm in love with Ella.

I loved Vivien, and a sad part of me will always love her, but it is Ella now and not Vivien that I think of every day. That I take to bed. That I crave. That I miss when we are not together. That I want to call and tell when something happens to me. That I want to share my life with.

Vivien's mother looks at me sadly. 'When I lost my daughter, I lost a son, too. You were the best thing that ever happened to my Viv. It was my greatest dream to see you both married. I've missed you greatly, Dom.'

'I'm sorry I didn't come round before today, Mirela. I always enjoyed our little chats.'

She smiles happily. 'Me too. You're like a son to me, Dom. You must come and see me again.'

'I will.'

'I've thought of you a lot. I know you've made a great success of your life. The ladies at the church.' She smiles shyly. 'I listen to their gossip.'

'Mirela,' I begin and then I pause.

'What is it, Dom?' she prompts.

'When Vivien was dying in the water, I made her a promise. I told her I would never love anyone else.'

'Oh, Dom. Have you let that promise keep you from finding happiness all these years?'

I link my fingers together and say nothing.

 228

She leans forward. 'Listen to me. She was afraid, and she was clinging on to you. I love my daughter, but she was a minx to make you promise such a thing. She's gone, and you are here. You've wasted ten years. Don't waste another moment. If there is one thing I learned from losing Vivien, it is to appreciate every moment you have with the people you love.' Her lips curl up in a bitter smile. 'You don't know how long you have with them.'

'I still feel guilty. I could have saved her.' I exhale my breath slowly. 'If we hadn't argued. If I hadn't told her Jake was coming.'

She starts shaking her head in distress. 'Don't do that, dear boy. There was nothing you could have done to stop it. God knows, you tried. It was simply her time.'

'She was too young to die.'

'About four months after Viv passed, I dreamed of her. In my dream she was eleven or twelve years old, before she started dyeing her hair in all those atrocious colors. She was running in a field and she was laughing. Her mouth was stained with the juice of berries. She ran up to me and said, "Look what I found, Mum." And then I woke up and I cried for hours.'

She pulls a handkerchief that she has tucked into her bra out from the neckline of her blouse and wipes her eyes.

'But as the weeks and months went by, I took comfort from that dream. I think she wanted me to know she wasn't blue and lying

in a satin-lined box as she was in my waking hours. She wasn't still. She wasn't dead. She was alive. Somewhere in another dimension that I can't access, she still exists. She has never appeared again in my dreams, but she doesn't need to. I understood what she was saying to me.'

'She's never come to me,' I say.

'Perhaps you are only allowed to go to the people you can no longer damage,' she says softly.

'I found someone,' I blurt out suddenly, but even as the words exit my mouth I want to un-utter them. I am shocked at myself. What madness possessed me to tell Viv's grieving mother *that*?

She swallows hard. 'I'm so glad,' she croaks.

Angry with myself, I apologize. 'I'm so sorry. That was unforgivably insensitive of me. I don't know what came over me.'

She shakes her head and, reaching out a work-worn hand, grips my knee. 'No, I'm glad for you. You're a good man. You deserve to be happy.'

I cover her hand with mine.

'You know that song by Pitball?' she asks.

I smile slightly. 'Pitbull?'

'Yes, yes, the man with the bald head.'

'You listen to Pitbull?' I ask, surprised.

'My granddaughter does.'

'Marko has a daughter now?'

230

'He has three children. Two boys and a girl. They're my life. Anyway, Pitbull sings a song called "Give Me Everything Tonight". He says, "What I promise tonight, I cannot promise tomorrow." That's truly life. You might not get tomorrow. So whatever you want to do, go do it tonight.'

And from her wise body precious memories flow into me. If not for the intervention of the cruel hand of fate, she would have been my mother-in-law. I squeeze her hand and feel a great love for this kind and generous woman. We are connected forever by having loved the same person, and by the grief of having lost her.

'When you remember Vivien, remember that she was always laughing, always wanting to have fun. She wouldn't want to be the barbed wire wrapped around your heart.'

I nodded. 'I know.'

I press a thick wad of money into her reluctant hand and kiss her powdered cheek goodbye. She stands at the door and gazes wistfully at me. I walk up to her wooden gate. I even open it. Then something pulls at me. I turn around and walk back to her. She looks at me enquiringly.

'I want to show you something, but I don't want to upset you,' I say.

'Yes, show me,' she says immediately.

I take my phone out and scroll to the picture of Ella. I hold the phone out to her. 'This is Ella, my girlfriend.' And in that moment I know that I love Ella with my entire being.

She gazes at the phone for a long time. When she looks up, her eyes are swimming with tears. 'She's beautiful, Dom. Will you bring her to dinner one day soon?'

I nod, and it's impossible for me to talk because I'm so choked up.

'God knew he shouldn't have taken her away from you,' she says, giving me back the phone.

I take the phone from her and walk away, my heart finally free.

Where, O death, is your victory:
where, O death, is your sting?
—1 Corinthians 15: 55

TWENTY-SIX

Dom

I turn the car around and drive to the cemetery where Vivien was laid to rest. It's a sunny day and the cemetery looks pretty with brightly colored petunias bordering it. I park and go up to a rickety iron gate. I'm not sure exactly where her grave is, but I remember my mother once mentioning that hers is a plot in the east end of the cemetery, and that there's an oak tree nearby.

I take one of the small paths that radiate out to a serpentine perimeter path to lead visitors around the outer graves, some of which are centuries old. It's hard to imagine that these people walked this earth hundreds of years ago.

They are mostly overgrown, unkempt and crumbling, but one of the ancient, ornate altar tombs catches my attention, and I find myself wandering to it, and reading the worn inscription. Herein lies Arthur Anderson-Black.

Resting in the arms of God forever,
loved forever, missed desperately.
Flying with the angels, your memory
will never die. Our beloved father,
brother and uncle. We will never forget you.
Rest in peace till we meet again.
1830–1875

I think of the mourners who erected the tombstone for him three hundred years ago. Their remains have joined his under the clay soil. But did they meet again? I've never walked around a cemetery on my own before, and it is an oddly surreal experience. Walking among the dead makes you appreciate the impermanence of life and the permanence of death like nothing else can. All these people once lived and walked and talked and did their thing as if they would live forever. This house is mine, this land is mine, and now they are all just gone forever.

The saddest headstones are the ones erected by grieving parents. They are the most poignant. A simple epitaph on a new grave touched me deeply.

Beneath this simple stone
that marks her resting place
our precious darling sleeps
alone in the Lord's long embrace.
May 2001–December 2001

As I stroll along the path I remember what my mother once told me. When the fruit is ripe and ready, it will leave the branch easily. I was the branch that Vivien was torn away from. I wasn't ready. She still had too much to live for. Without realizing it I have fallen into a kind of melancholy, contemplative mood, and it is a shock to see a hilarious marble tombstone.

Is This Headstone Tax Deductible?

It makes me smile. I take my phone out and take a photo for Ella. The tax inspector in her will appreciate it.

The curved outer path meets an axial pathway that takes me to a central chapel, and a small custodian's lodge that was designed to be used for burial services. The path meanders, and I pass a newly dug grave awaiting its occupant.

I walk over to the manicured grass and spot the oak tree in the distance. I begin to walk toward it. I no longer look at the gravestones on either side of me. As if I'm guided by an invisible hand, I move forward with sure steps until I'm standing in front of Vivien's grave. My breath escapes in a long sigh. Ah, Vivien. Her grave is a custom memorial in polished black granite with a carved weeping angel holding a rose. The setting sun makes the stone glow red.

Vivien Jessica Finch

Goodnight, dear heart,
goodnight, goodnight
Oct, 10, 1987–Jul, 24, 2004

I kneel down and touch the smooth stone. How she would have hated this place. This peace. This quiet. This impenetrable air of mourning and stillness. The impulsive, impetuous Vivien with roses in her hair, the one who could never sit still for a moment is not here. I laugh. The sound is loud and strange among the silent tombstones. It disturbs the peace. Perhaps no one has laughed here in centuries.

A strong breeze rushes at my face. I look up, surprised. And suddenly I hear Vivien saying, 'I'll come back and haunt you.'

'You never did come back to haunt me, did you?' I whisper into the wind.

And I remember her laughing. How she used to laugh. She was wild and beautiful, but never vindictive.

I wonder where she is now.

'Wherever you are, Vivien, remember I truly loved you,' I say, and, in the trees, a lone bird calls. I stay a little while longer, but I am restless. For I stand there, a living, breathing mortal, with hot blood flowing in my veins. One day I'll join them in their repose and their silence, but not yet. I have a life and it's calling me. I walk away and never look back.

As soon as I get into my car, I call Ella. She picks up on the first ring.

'Ella,' I say.

And she starts to weep.

And suddenly I can't wait to see her. 'Where are you?' I ask.

'On the way home,' she sobs.

'Go home and wait for me. I'm taking you out to dinner. I'll be there in less than an hour. Wear something sexy,' I say, joy pouring through my living blood.

I stuff my phone into my pocket and, feeling light-hearted enough to fly, I run up the three flights of stairs. I let myself into my flat and, pressing my palms to my face, I go to the mirror. Wow! Look at me glow.

Undressing quickly, I step into the shower. I fly out in five minutes and do my hair. Putting a tiny amount of gel into the ends of my hair I blow dry it, and leave it as a mass of tumbling curls on my back and shoulders.

Then I sit on the bed and paint my toenails bright fuchsia. I wait ten minutes for them to dry. When they are, I pull on strawberry-flavored, edible panties, carefully stick edible, chocolate-flavored arrow tattoos

on my belly and thighs. All arrows point towards my hoo-ha, which has already started humming with anticipation.

Oh, and there are watermelon-flavored pasties for my nipples.

Just thinking of Dom licking everything off makes a shiver run down my back. Smiling happily, I slip into a white dress with secret mesh panels on the bodice and back. It molds to my body then flares out from mid-thigh to my ankles.

With butterflies in my tummy, I step into strappy silver shoes. My toenails, bright and glossy, peep out as I walk three times into a cloud of perfume I have sprayed above my head. Sitting at the dressing table, I apply fuchsia lipstick and a layer of mascara, and I'm ready. I look at the time. Still ten minutes to go. The doorbell rings. He's early. He's eager. I grin at my reflection.

Way to go, girl.

I don't walk to answer the door, I run. I open the door and my smile dies on my lips. I recognized him straightaway, even with the unkempt beard and mustache, but why on earth is he dressed like that? And what the hell is he doing here? What's that supermarket trolley doing out in the corridor? But before I can say or do anything he reaches out, and stabs me in the hand with something sharp that he was holding concealed.

It acts so quickly I don't even feel myself hit the floor.

TWENTY-SEVEN

I, stalker

'Do not run away; let go. Do not seek, for it will come when least expected.'

—

Bruce Lee

Quickly, I push the trolley into her apartment and close the door. Using the tattered blankets inside the trolley, I bundle her up in them. Then I turn the trolley on its side, and pull out all the assorted bits and pieces inside it: old newspapers, empty tins, plastic bottles, some boxes. I drag the trolley so it's facing her body and kind of roll and push her body into it.

Excellent ... She fits even better than I thought.

Grunting, I try to pull the trolley upright, but it is too heavy. I let it drop back down. Slight change of plans. Straightening, I walk over to a small, painted cabinet and take

out a phone directory. I lift the trolley slightly and push the thick book into the gap. Now I have more leverage. Using both hands I give the trolley another great heave. My second attempt is successful.

Panting slightly, I throw the other odds and ends on top of her body and stand back to look at the end effect critically. Yes, no one would suspect that it is anything other than the trolley of a homeless man filled with everything he possesses. There's a mirror on her wall and I go and look at myself.

Good. I look like a tramp—unwashed, unshaven, dirty. It took me weeks to perfect this look. Because of her, I've spent every waking moment planning and learning. Yes, I learned to pick locks, to gather intel, to bug, to follow, to immerse myself into my disguises, to pretend to be Melanie, someone who likes and makes light-hearted comments on all her pathetic little posts on Facebook.

Carefully, I push the trolley into the lift. Thank God! It's working.

As I push her through the foyer, I see the big man go running up the stairs. And I smile. Too late! I push her out into the evening air and down the street. Not one person looks me in the eye or suspects anything. By the time I get to my basement flat it's nearly dark. I glance around. There's not a soul about.

I go down the steps and open the front door of the place I have rented. I go back up and overturn the trolley. I pull her body out

and carry her down to my flat, her feet dragging against every step it takes to get to my front door. I drop her inert body just inside my house and, running up the stairs, I push the trolley down the steps and leave it in my garden. Then I go back into my house and close my front door.

There, there now. All done.

It is destiny that she should fall into my hands like an apple from a tree.

I drag her to a wall and prop her into a sitting position against it. The harsh illumination from the bare single light bulb makes her skin glow. Up close, she is even more beautiful. It's obvious that she doesn't belong in these surroundings. Her perfume wafts up to my nostrils. I breathe it in deeply. I haven't smelt a woman for a long time. Not one as fine as her, anyway. My hand moves to her breasts, but I can't bring myself to touch her. No, I won't steal it when she's asleep. I'm not lustful and unchaste. She'll be bound, naked and wide-awake, when I defile her.

She must witness the moment I force myself on her, and bring her to ruin.

I secure her hands behind her back with plastic ties. Next, her legs. Rolling her onto her side, I look at her. Her face is angelic. It's almost an abomination to see her silky golden curls tumble onto the dirty carpet. I used to dream of them spread over my thighs as she swallowed my cock.

Bitch ruined my life.

I spit in the dirt near her head and move away from her.

In that first moment of consciousness, when it's still dark behind my eyelids, there is only the sensation of a throbbing pain in my temples. The sensations that follow on are much stranger. An unfamiliar feeling of stiffness and constriction. Something scratchy against my cheek. The smell of damp and dirt. My eyes snap open in alarm. My hands and legs are tightly bound, and I'm lying on my side on a filthy carpet. My mind goes blank. What the hell is happening? I blink, and lift my head from the rough bristles.

'You're awake,' a man's voice says.

And it all comes flooding back.

Oh God!

My blood runs cold. A pair of jeans-clad legs and badly stained sneakers come into view. I raise my frightened eyes all the way up to his face. Oh, dear Jesus! My mouth opens.

'Surprise!' he says.

My voice is hoarse; a shocked whisper. 'What are you doing?'

Rob's cold, mean eyes regard me steadily, pitilessly.

'What do you want from me?' I cry desperately.

The question seems to infuriate him. His eyes flash, but he controls himself. 'What do you think I want?' he asks menacingly.

I stare at him with startled, terrified eyes.

'I know you like big cocks. I've watched you take it all into your dirty cunt. All of it being stuffed into Ella Savage's greedy, greedy cunt,' he says in a sing-song voice.'

'Please, Sir,' I say automatically, my mind and eyes unable to believe the transformation of the man I knew for more than a year to this dirty, crazed man and the hateful words that are pouring from his mouth. How could he have hidden this from me? From all of us?

His eyes widen mockingly. 'You don't have to beg, Ella. You're a dirty bitch but I'll fuck you.'

I shake my head to clear it, but it causes a flash of pain to stab at my temples. I'm too confused to be able to comprehend my situation. I look at him pleadingly. 'Why are you doing this? I haven't done anything bad to you.'

'You know,' he says evenly. 'You are the most self-absorbed bitch I have ever had the misfortune to meet. I was *in love* with you, you shameless slut.'

'What?' It is like being in the twilight zone. Nothing makes sense. Rob was in love with me!

'Unbelievable! She didn't even notice,' he notes in wonder.

'How was I to know?' I cry defensively. 'You were always rude and cold to me.'

'If I had not been rude and cold would you have loved me back?'

Oh, my God. Oh, my God. I'll never be able to reason with him. 'Maybe.'

He walks up to me and viciously kicks me in the stomach. The wind is knocked out of me. I gasp for breath and automatically curl myself protectively, but there are no more blows. I need a strategy. I need to keep him from getting angrier. I need to calm him down.

'That's for lying. No more lies.' He stands over me. 'Have I made myself clear?'

Unable to speak I nod.

'You haven't answered the question.'

I turn my face and look him in the eye. 'No.'

He explodes with laughter, a bitter sound that rings around the empty flat. 'I thought so. Too good for me, are you?'

'No,' I try to explain. 'You were my boss. I never even thought about you like that.'

He turns his back to me, his palms clasped over his head, before suddenly swiveling around to face me, grotesquely

angry. 'You didn't think of me like that,' he shouts. 'Do you know that I've been taking care of you and protecting you from the moment you appeared for the interview all round-eyed and dewy faced. You were never good enough for the job, too weak and indecisive, but I took you in, taught you everything, and gave you a chance. And what do you do? At the first opportunity you turn your back on me for that stinking gypsy brute.'

He spits on the ground.

'By the time I came back from the toilet it was already too late, wasn't it? You were itching for his dick. All the way back to the office in the car, I could smell your arousal. Disgusting.'

My mind scrambles around wildly. I have to pacify him. 'It's not like that,' I tell him, my voice trembling with emotion. 'I didn't turn my back on you. I quit my job because I found out we were wrong about everything. We've all been manipulated and tricked into demonizing the wrong sections of society. The real cheats, the truly rich, are always going to be out of our reach, and all we are doing is squeezing the ordinary person.'

He narrows his eyes. 'How convenient! As soon as you landed yourself a loaded boyfriend, you're no longer interested in protecting the poor, taxpaying public anymore, and become more concerned with not demonizing the section of society he belongs to.'

I exhale in frustration. 'You don't understand. I truly believed we were helping the ordinary hard-working British public, preventing them from having their pockets picked by people who didn't pay their proper taxes, but he showed me that I was wrong.'

He pushes out his jaw aggressively. 'I can't believe I wasted all that time on you. You're just a stupid bitch.'

'I'm sorry. I'm really sorry. I honestly didn't mean to hurt you,' I cry out.

He stares at me, his face hard. 'It's great that you're sorry, but it doesn't change a damn thing for me. I've got nothing because of you. Did you know I was happily married? She used to make steak and kidney pies for me on Sundays. And then you came, batted your eyelashes, made me want you, and ruined everything.' He runs his hands through his hair distractedly. 'I've done things for you. I even took care of Michael for you'

'You did what?' I gasp.

'Yes, I broke into his house and made those phone calls so you could actually have the necessary proof and get your restraining order.'

My mouth drops open. 'He never stalked me, did he?'

'He didn't have the brains to be a stalker,' he scoffed. 'That was me. It was always me. I was always loyal to you.'

'Where is Michael now? Have you done something to him?'

'Of course not. I'm not a killer. Well, I wasn't. You are the only one capable of driving me to murder.'

He squats next to me. His crotch is so close to my face I can smell his odor: an unwashed, stale, cheesy smell. He flicks open a switchblade and brings it close to my face. It catches the light and inspires dread. Averting my gaze from it, I realize that he's just trying to frighten me, but I can't help the terror that floods my entire body. He's a man who has driven himself to the edge of madness. And he's holding a knife.

'Look at you. You thought you could say sorry and all would be forgiven.' Reaching out a hand he puts it on my bare knee.

I flinch. 'Please. Please don't,' I beg.

His eyes are cold. 'Don't worry. I don't have a big cock. I will fit beautifully in your ass.'

I shake my head with terror.

He bends closer, his eyes widening menacingly. 'Don't you like it up the ass? Didn't the slimy gypsy stuff his dick up your bottom?'

'I'm sorry. I'm so sorry. I didn't mean to hurt you,' I cry.

'No, I'm sure you didn't mean it. However, you did. And now you can compensate me for my suffering,' he says, and slowly runs his hand up the inside of my thigh.

I squeeze my legs shut and trap his hand. He laughs, an ugly sound. He wrenches his hand out from between my thighs and continues upwards on the fronts of my thighs. His progress is relentless. His fingers have already reached the edible panties that I wore especially for Dom. I stare at him desperately. His fingers suddenly pinch my pussy lips together and I jump with horror.

At that, lust filters into his eyes. With both hands, he tears my skirt right to my waist. He sees the chocolate arrows and a light comes into his eyes.

'My, my, what do we have here?'

He bends his head and licks an arrow.

I start screaming, but he suddenly slaps me so hard my jaw feels like it has been dislocated. Stinging tears fill my eyes.

He grabs my panties.

My head and jaw are throbbing so bad I can hardly open my mouth. 'Wait,' I cry, a sharp pain shuddering through my face.

His hand stills.

'Yes, my thoughtless actions brought you terrible pain. But are you better than me if you rape me?'

IIis eyes flicker. 'I'll pay for my sins. But now it's your turn. Don't worry I'm kind enough to use butter.'

I draw in a shocked breath.

'I don't want to tear you. I want to use you many times before I discard you.'

'And after you've raped me, what will you do? Kill me? And then what?'

He takes his hand off my thigh. 'Don't you get it? The only thing left for me is the satisfaction of knowing you will get what you deserve.'

He turns me roughly onto my front.

'Pleeeeease,' I beg.

He hooks his fingers into the top of my flimsy, edible panties. At that moment there is a massive bang and the door of the dingy flat flies open and hits the wall hard. Both Rob and I freeze. Dom charges through the door followed by Jake. Even through the fear and shock my brain notes that they look so big and ferocious compared to Rob. Before I know it, I feel the cold, sharp end of Rob's knife pressing into the skin of my throat.

'Don't come any closer, or I'll slit this bitch's throat from ear to ear,' he threatens with a tremor of panic in his voice.

Both Dom and Jake take a step back, Dom with both his hands raised, the palms showing.

Jake is the first to speak. 'If you hurt her, we will kill you. If you let her go now, you have my word we'll do nothing to you. We won't go to the police. We're gypsies—we settle everything on our own. I'll even give you money.'

'Money,' Rob spits. 'You think you can buy me? This is *my* bitch.'

I see Dom start, his face reddens, and his hands clench so hard the muscles of his shoulders bulge.

'Listen,' Jake says. 'If you think you're going to walk out of here alive after touching one hair on her head you're mad.'

My breathing is shallow. Rob's painfully firm grip on my shoulder has not eased at all.

I feel Rob's body become tense. In the end he is a coward.

'You'll gain nothing by taking a life and surrendering your own. Make no mistake. If you harm her, we'll kill you with our bare hands.'

Rob's grip eases a fraction.

'Let her go. We won't hurt you,' Jake adds persuasively.

'You'll not keep your word. I know how this works.'

Dom is as still as a statue.

'No. My word is my honor,' Jake says.

Rob's face crumples. Suddenly, he erupts with the hysterical laughter of a madman. Nobody reacts. Both Dom and Jake remain stony-faced. As suddenly as he had begun laughing, he stops. 'All right. Prove it,' he says, and throws the knife on the ground.

No sooner does the knife hit the ground than Dom rushes forward with an incoherent cry of rage and starts kicking the shit out of Rob. In his uncontrollable frenzy, strings of curses stream out of his snarling mouth. 'You fucking ugly cunt. You think you're so big? Let's see how big you are without your blade. Fucking piece of chicken shit.'

Jake grabs Dom by the front of his shirt and pushes him back.

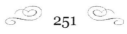

'Look at her face. He fucking hit her. I want to kill the fucking cunt,' Dom roars.

'No, you fucking don't,' Jake growls. 'Take your woman out of this hellhole and leave me with him.'

Dom's face is tight and tense, and his hands are clenched into fists. He takes a great shuddering breath as he fights to control his natural instinct.

Jake lets go of his shirt. 'Go home, Dom.'

Dom turns toward me, his face immediately softening. Taking his jacket off, he covers my half-naked body with it. While Rob cowers on the ground and Jake stands over him, Dom takes the knife from the floor and cuts the ties around my hands and ankles. Then he takes me into his arms and hugs me tightly.

'Come on,' he says in my ear.

I pull away from him. He stands and pulls me up. My legs are shaking. He puts his arm around my back, and leads me out of that hellhole.

TWENTY-EIGHT

Jake

I wait for the door to close then I walk over to the man curled up and writhing on the floor. I stop in front of him and he looks up at me with bulging eyes.

'Please, I beg you. Don't hurt me. I'll do whatever you ask,' he whines like the coward that he is.

I yank him up, struggling, cowering and screaming like a stuck pig, and pin him against the wall, until he suddenly realizes I am not going to hurt him, yet. I let go of him so he falls to the floor. He lands in a heap, but quickly scrambles into a sitting position against the wall. I fix my eyes on his bloodied face. His left eye is beginning to swell, his cheek is grazed and there is a cut on his lip which is bleeding.

The knife is beside us. His bulging eyes stray to it, and I don't try to kick it out of the way or reach for it. Instead I smile coldly and instantly his mouth begins to tremble uncontrollably.

'You gave your word,' he grovels.

Calmly I reach down and pick up the knife.

'What are you doing?' he cries in panic. He is so terrified he is trying to crawl sideways up the wall.

I move close enough to hear his heart thumping in its cage and say nothing. Simply watch the terror behind his pupils. Taking my time, I bring the knife to his throat and point it so the tip nicks his throat. He freezes. A drop of blood appears on his skin.

'Please, please, don't kill me. I wasn't going to hurt her. I just wanted to frighten her, teach her a lesson. I love her,' he begs pathetically.

I frown. 'You don't love her. You can't. You're a rat. She's a woman. Rats don't love human beings.'

'Yes, yes, I'm a rat. You're right. I don't love her,' he agrees immediately, shaking his head wildly, snot running from his nose and into his mouth.

'So we both understand this clearly. Whose woman is Ella?'

'Your brother's,' he utters immediately

I inhale the stench of his urine. A dark stain is spreading over his crotch. I raise my eyes back to his blubbering face and feel nothing. Not even hatred. He could be a discarded bottle top on the floor of one of my clubs. A bit of waste. A nuisance. I have to pay someone to clean it up, dispose of it.

'Good. I'm glad we agree. Now. You made a mistake when you took my brother's woman, because that involves me and a whole world of trouble for you,' I tell him.

Sheer panic leeches into his face. It's been a long, long time since I brought a man to such fear. It's irritating that I have to do this. I don't want to be like this. But men like him force me to return to this unpleasant business.

My voice is emotionless and flat. 'My brother isn't a killer. Sure, you got his blood boiling, but a kicking within an inch of your life is as far as it would have gone. Me, I can kill in cold blood. I could kill you right now without breaking into a sweat. As painless as swatting a fly.'

His head jerks.

I continue as if we are having a polite conversation. 'There are so many ways I could end it for you. Slit an artery and watch you bleed out on this floor. My favorite, actually. Or stab you repeatedly, slicing through every vital organ. A bit messy, but it has its uses. Or many non-fatal cuts to make you suffer a long, slow painful death. So far no one has pissed me off enough to make me resort to this method yet.'

He shudders visibly.

'I would probably be doing the world a favor to kill you, but looks like you're the luckiest man alive tonight. We arrived here

before you had a chance to really fuck it up for yourself. So I'm going to make this one exception. I'm going to let you live. I am going to walk out of here and you are going back to wherever you presently call home. Once you get there you have twenty-four hours to put your affairs into order and leave London. For-fucking-ever!'

I nod slowly.

'I don't care where you go or how you get there. Take a flight, take a boat, take a train, but in twenty-fours if you are still anywhere within 100 miles of my brother, *his* woman, her family or me, you will have a sea burial. There are two men outside. They will follow you home. Don't mind them. They won't harm you. Their job is to escort you home safely.'

I stop and pause. 'Do you understand me?'

He nods so violently his head bangs against the wall.

He reaches out a hand towards my leg, 'Thank—.'

My voice is like a whiplash. For the first time I actually feel enough raw fury to end his life. 'Don't even fucking go there,' I tell him.

He shrinks and begins coughing and spluttering.

'Good.' I stand and look down at him for a few seconds longer, and then I turn away and open the door. I take the stone steps two at a time and see the car with my

back-up pair, Eddy and Mace inside. Eddie lifts his hand. I nod. As I step onto the pavement my phone rings. It's Lily.

'Hey, baby,' I say into the phone. And there is nothing but love in my voice.

TWENTY-NINE

Ella

Dom opens the passenger door to a blue Mercedes-Benz sedan and I slide in. I want to ask whose car it is, but I don't. I feel too numb and cold to actually care. Some part of me is still in that disgusting flat, still with Rob. Yes, I was so afraid of him.

I turn to Dom urgently.

'What will Jake do to Rob?'

'I hope he kills that miserable fucking coward,' he rages.

'I don't want him to be killed,' I whisper.

He turns on me. 'Why do you care so much? Fucking hell, Ella, he had a knife to your throat and he'd already torn your skirt.' He clenches his jaw. 'God knows what he would have done if we'd not come when we did!'

'I don't want his blood on my conscience, Dom. Please,' I say with a sob.

 258

His face softens. He grabs my forearms and pulls me toward him. 'Listen. Jake is honorable in the old-fashioned way. In the gypsy way. But he'll arrange it so that pathetic pussy never comes near you again.'

I start to cry softly. 'Just take me home, please.'

'Hey. Don't cry, baby. You're safe now,' he cajoles, and pulls me tight against his chest, careful not to hurt my throbbing jaw.

'Just take me home,' I whisper tearfully into the hollow of his throat.

He takes me home and parks outside the entrance.

'You'll get a ticket,' I warn automatically.

'It doesn't matter,' he says, and, getting out of the car, helps me out. Together we walk up the three flights of stairs. When we get upstairs, I realize that I have no keys. I look up at him. My head is spinning, my jaw is throbbing and I can't think properly.

'I don't have my keys,' I wail as if it's the end of the world.

'It's OK, Ella. I have mine,' he says gently.

He lets me in. I stand in the hallway of my little home. The first thing I see is the phone book on the floor. I can't understand why it is there. I look around me. Everything is the same, and yet everything is different. It has been invaded by a man who hates me. The thought makes me feel almost ill. I press my lips together to stop from breaking into tears again.

'I need to take a shower,' I say in a trembling voice, and start walking toward the bathroom. Dom catches me and tugs me back so I'm pressed up against his body.

He takes my chin in his hand.

'I feel so dirty,' I say.

'You're not dirty, Ella. We got to you before anything really bad could happen.'

I frown. 'How did you find me so quickly?'

He curls his hand around my wrist and lifts it up to my eye level.

'What?' I ask, confused.

'This is a chipped bracelet.'

'What?' I say, confused.

'Told you I was a paranoid motherfucker.'

'You gave me a bracelet with a tracking chip and you never told me about it?' I ask incredulously.

'Yeah,' he says, totally unfazed.

I pull slightly away from him. 'And you've been tracking me all this time?'

'Not really. The chip is in there, but while you were safe there was no need to track you.'

'I can't believe you gave me a chipped bracelet, like I'm your pet or something.'

'You're my woman. I protect what's mine,' he says forcefully.

I shake my head in disbelief. I want to be angry, but I'm all emotioned out. I look at

the bracelet that he gave me two weeks ago. Gold with little square pieces of sapphire set into it. It's a bloody tracking device. Still, I can't complain, it certainly came in handy today.

'I know about Vivien,' I say softly. My heart feels as if it's a heavy rock.

'I know. Jake told me.'

I sniff and look at the pulse beating steadily in his throat. 'I saw a picture of her,' I say, trying to be casual, and failing miserably.

He puts his finger under my chin and lifts it until I'm forced to look into his gorgeous eyes. They are filled with soft lights, the pupils so large they are almost the size of his irises. 'Yeah, you look like her. And yeah, I admit, in the beginning I confused my lust for you with a love lost tragically. I thought you'd make the pain go away for a while. I thought I was temporarily re-creating an old magic. I didn't know you were a thief. That you'd steal my heart, weave yourself into my soul, and make me fall deeper in love with you than I've ever done with anyone else.'

My mouth drops open. 'You ... love me?'

'Yes.' He beams.

I shake my head in disbelief. 'You love *me*?'

'Yes, I love you, Ella Savage. I fucking love you.'

'Since when?' I ask, almost unable to believe what he is telling me.

'I don't know. All I know is that I love, love, love you.' He picks me up and twirls me around. 'And I'm never letting you go.'

I look down at him seriously. 'Maybe you just think you love me because I look like Vivien?'

'Oh, my darling, darling Ella. You've no idea. I'm so in love with you, I feel high, as if I've dropped an ecstasy tablet.'

'But how do you know it's really me you want and not her?' I insist.

'No two women could be more different than you and Vivien. It's you I want to wake up to in the morning. It's your skin I crave, and it's your laughter I yearn to hear on the phone.'

'Oh, Dom. I feel so confused. I don't know what's happening anymore. First, I find out about Vivien, then I get kidnapped, then I think I'm going to be sodomized and raped, and then I get rescued, and now you're telling me you love me! I'm thinking I'm going to wake up soon!'

'Want me to pinch you?' His eyes light up. 'Or, better still, I can fuck you awake? Did I see a chocolate arrow on your thigh just now?'

I have a sudden image of Rob, his long, hot tongue slowly licking the other chocolate arrow from my thigh. I shudder. 'I need a shower.'

His face hardens. 'Did he do anything to you?'

'No,' I deny immediately. 'Of course not.'

'Then how come there's only one chocolate arrow?' he demands aggressively.

Suddenly tears come back to my eyes. 'Please, Dom. Leave him alone. If he is diseased, I infected him.'

'Did he do anything to you? I'll fucking kill the sick bastard if he did,' he declares furiously.

I take both his hands in my palms and look deep into his eyes. 'No, Dom. He didn't do anything to me. After everything that's happened, I just feel unclean. I need to wash my body and my hair.'

'All right,' he says. 'Want me to come with you?'

'No. Why don't you pour yourself a drink? I'll be out soon.'

I go into the bathroom and take all my clothes off and stand under the hot shower. I rub at the chocolate arrow vigorously. Then I see the watermelon pasties run pink into the plughole and I start to cry. I don't know why I'm crying. Maybe it's the tension. I hear a noise, and the door to the shower is open and one hot, fully erect alpha is standing there.

'Don't cry, Ella' he says softly. 'You're safe now.'

'I know,' I sniff.

And he puts out a hand and touches my midriff where a huge bruise has formed. 'He hurt you,' he whispers in a shocked voice.

'It actually doesn't hurt.' And it's true.

He comes into the shower, and the cubicle is so small the practical solution is for me to climb onto his body and curl my legs around him while he holds on to my buttocks and fucks me. Hard. Oh, so hard. It's what I need. I feel the tension, fear and doubt wash away. We come together under the cascading water. He kisses me gently and I cling on to my hero. God, he's so gorgeous.

'This weekend I'm taking you riding. You'll love it.'

'Why? Because Vivien loved it?'

He smiles, a beautiful, pure smile. 'No, because it's horses. You cannot *not* love my horses.'

'OK.' I grin.

'Do you love me?' he asks.

'Oh, Hell!' I say. 'Isn't that as obvious as fuck?'

'Yeah, it is, but I just like to hear it rolling off your tongue,' he says with a mischievous, awesome, sexy grin.

And we both laugh.

I can be your hero, baby
https://www.youtube.com/watch?v=ko
JlIGDImiU

EPILOGUE

SIX MONTHS LATER

I lift the stick and see the thin blue line. And a bubble of laughter comes up and erupts in my mouth. Oh, my God. Oh, my God. I put the stick on the edge of the sink, wash my hands, and walking on air, go back into the bedroom.

'Come here, woman,' Dom says from the bed.

I don't go to him. I just stand there and admire him. His swarthy skin contrasting darkly against the white sheet. His chest and arms muscular. His smile white and beautiful. A thought. I can't believe he is really mine. I wake up every morning and I just can't believe my luck. Nobody gets this lucky, surely?

He raises his body up slightly, his smile disappearing. 'What's wrong?'

I smile happily. 'Nothing. Absolutely nothing.'

'So what're you standing there for? I'm hungry for pussy juice.'

I laugh and go forward. He reaches out and pulls me into bed and I tumble into his warm, hard body.

'What's this?' I say with widened eyes.

'That, Mrs. Eden is called your husband's fucking erect cock.'

While I am still laughing, he rolls me over on my back. I feel a finger slide into me. I stop laughing. 'Oh, Dom,' I sigh.

A long time later, when we are both exhausted and lying on our side facing each other, he says, 'I did warn you I was hungry.'

'Mmmm,' I say sleepily.

'It's Sunday. Let's stay in bed and fuck and eat junk food all day.'

'I can't I promised my mother I'd help her pack.'

He is immediately on his elbow looking down at me, a frown line between his eyebrows. 'Pack? Pack what?'

'Her stuff. Remember they are moving in a week's time.'

'Fucking hell, Ella. My wife doesn't pack. That's what movers are for. Shit, you could ruin your back doing things like that.'

'I have called the company you told me to call. They are packing all the big things. I'm just helping Mum to package some of her decorative items in bubble wrap.'

I touch his face wonderingly. 'Thank you for taking care of my parents. My Mum thinks she died and went to heaven. Not even in her wildest dreams did she think she could ever own a house, let alone something so beautiful as the one you bought them. And my father is a whole different man. Who knew that all he needed was hormone therapy?'

'I'm the one who has to thank them for giving you to me,' he says lovingly.

'Talking about that. You might be in a position of giving someone away too in about twenty odd years.'

He suddenly rolls me over and pins me under him. 'You're still speaking English, right?'

I burst out laughing. 'Yes, I am.'

He frowns. 'It's not going to be able to crawl as fast as Tommy, or speak like Liliana is it?'

I laugh even more. 'I don't know it might.'

'Oh shit,' he curses.

'Stop making a joke of everything, you big fucking hulk, you. Aren't you happy?'

He looks down at me, blue eyes full of laughter. 'Yes, I'm so happy I could fuck you all over again.'

I grin up happily at him.

'I love you, Ella.'

A warm feeling of such love and joy gushes into me I have to gasp. 'I love you too,

Dominic Eden. I love you so much I could fuck you all over again.

'Go on then,' he challenges cheekily, as his mouth comes down to claim me.

EIGHTEEN MONTHS LATER

Dom

I place Adam on the changing mat.

'Right,' I say confidently. 'Let's do this.'

He gurgles up at me. I take a deep breath and blow it out.

'Right,' I say again. 'We're doing it without Mummy.'

This time he blows a bubble. I look down on the changing mat.

Wipes. Check.

Fresh clean diaper. Check.

Diaper rash cream. Check.

Plastic bag for disposing of soiled diaper. Check.

If I'm really fast I won't get more than a lungful of stench. Adam kicks his legs and hands encouragingly. I unfold a diaper and put it close by.

Gently, I take his shoes and socks off. He seems happy enough at this stage, and so am I. I unbutton his little suit and expose the diaper. I pull his little legs out of the suit.

I take a deep breath of clean air and, holding it in my lungs, I pull both the Velcro tabs at the same time, and, detaching the diaper from his tummy, reveal the extent of the damage.

Fuck! Not good.

I grab his ankles in my hand, pull his bottom upwards, and, using the diaper, wipe away the worst of the brown mess before smoothly sliding the diaper out. I fold it on itself and fix it with the sticky tapes. As fast as I can, I clean the area with the baby wipes, making sure to get into all the folds. I dump the wipes into the plastic bag with the soiled diaper and tie it tightly.

I let out the breath I was holding in a sudden burst.

Adam grabs his toes with his hands and watches the great big gulps of air I take.

'And then what happened?' I say to him.

He claps his hands and coos.

'Mummy's the first best thing that ever happened to me, and you're the second best thing that ever happened to me,' I tell him.

He lets out a little squeal.

'I know, but Mummy has to come first. Without Mummy there would be no Adam. You see how all this works, huh?'

I carry on talking more nonsense while I apply diaper cream, and then I lift his little bottom up again and slide the new diaper under him. I pull it over and snap the Velcro bits down. I dress him again in the same clothes. I tickle the soles of his feet and he cackles with laughter, his big blue eyes sparkling with innocence.

'You wait until you become a daddy. Then we'll see how you get on with changing dirty diapers.'

I wipe my hands and, picking him up, hold him close to my chest. After a big kiss and hug, we go downstairs. He can have a bottle of lovely warm milk while I have my glass of whiskey.

I've fucking earned it.

I open the door and see Dom coming down carrying Adam. My face breaks into a happy grin. No matter how many times I see the two of them together the joy that fills my heart never lessens. I love them both so much sometimes it feels as if my heart will burst with happiness.

'Hello,' I say.

'Ah, Mummy's home,' Dom says with a grin.

'Hello darling,' I say going closer to them. Adam is so crazy about his Dad he will

not come to me or anyone else when his father is around, but he does make an excited squawk and wave his little arms at me. I walk up to them and standing on tip- toes kiss first Dom and then my beautiful son.

I touch Adam's diaper. 'Does he need changing?'

'All done.'

My eyebrows rise. 'You changed his diaper?'

'Of course.'

I hide a smile. 'Any ... um ... problems?'

'No,' he says casually.

'Well done,' I say with a huge smile.

'Although, you really should stop feeding our son dead cats.'

I laugh.

'And what have you been up to?' he asks.

I lift up my bag of shopping. 'I got you your favourite.'

His eyes twinkle. 'Chocolate arrows?'

I pretend to be serious. 'No.'

'Watermelon pasties.'

'Be serious, you,' I reprimand with mock seriousness.

'If it's not watermelon pasties I give up. I don't know. What?'

'Edible panties.'

He grins cheekily. After thousands and thousands of grins. After all this time my tummy still flutters with the incredulous thought, and this man is mine?

'Wonderful,' he says, eyes twinkling. 'It's been ages since I ate one of those delicious things.'

'You ate one two weeks ago,' I remind.

'That's way too long, Ella, my love. Way too long.'

THE END

If you enjoyed Wounded Beast and want to know Jake's story, you'll find it here:

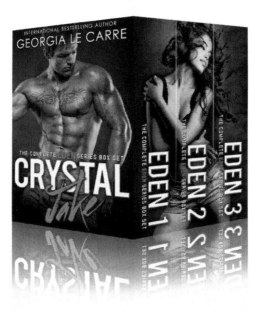

Amazon US:
http://www.amazon.com/dp/B00X2JUCRC
Amazon
UK: http://www.amazon.co.uk/gp/product/B00X2JU
CRC

Canada: http://www.amazon.ca/gp/product/B00X2J
UCRC
Amazon Aus:
http://www.amazon.com.au/gp/product/B00X2JUC
RC

Curious about BJ and Layla? Their love story is here:

http://www.amazon.com/Sexy-Beast-Gypsy-Heroes-.../.../B012GRLQJI
http://www.amazon.co.uk/gp/product/B012GRLQJI
http://www.amazon.com.au/Sexy-Beast-Georgia-Le.../.../B012GRLQJI
http://www.amazon.ca/gp/product/B012GRLQJI

SEXY BEAST

International Bestselling Author

GEORGIA LE CARRE

I **LOVE** hearing from my readers so by all means come and say hello here:
https://www.facebook.com/georgia.lecarre

or

Click on the link below to receive news of my latest releases, great giveaways, and exclusive content.
http://bit.ly/10e9WdE

On another note... :-)

Want To Help An Author?

Please leave a review. Reviews help other readers find an author's work. No matter how short it may be, it is very *precious. Links for your Amazon store below.*

Thank you!

http://www.amazon.com/dp/B012GRLQJI
http://www.amazon.co.uk/dp/B012GRLQJI

http://www.amazon.com.au/gp/produ
ct/B012GRLQJI
http://www.amazon.ca/gp/product/B
012GRLQJI

Coming Soon...

GOLD DIGGER

Georgia Le Carre

CHAPTER 1

'**W**hatever you do, don't *ever* trust them. Not one of them,' he whispered. His voice was so feeble I had to strain to catch it.

'I won't,' I said, softly.

'They are dangerous in a way you will never understand. Never let your guard down,' he insisted.

'I understand,' I said, but all I wanted was for him to stop talking about them. These last precious minutes I didn't want to waste on them.

He shook his head unhappily. 'No, no, you don't understand. You can never let your guard down for even an instant. Never.'

'All right, I won't.'

'I will be a very sad spirit if you do.'

'I won't,' I promised vehemently, and reached for his hand. The contrast between my hand and his couldn't have been greater. Mine was smooth and soft and his was gnarled and full of green veins, the skin waxy and liver-spotted. The nails were the color of polished ivory. The hand of a seventy-year-old man. His fingers grasped fiercely at my hand. I lifted them to my lips and kissed them one by one, tenderly.

His eyes glowed briefly in his wasted, sunken face. 'How I love you, my darling Tawny,' he murmured.

'I love you. I love you. I love you,' I said.

'Do your part and they cannot touch you.'

He sighed. 'It's nearly time.'

'Don't say that,' I cried, even though I knew in my heart that he was right.

His eyes swung to the window. 'Ah,' he sighed softly. 'You've come.'

My gaze chased his. The window he was looking at was closed, the heavy drapes pulled shut. Goose pimples crawled up my arms. 'Don't go yet. Please,' I begged.

He dragged his gaze reluctantly from the window. His thin, pale lips rose at the edges as he drew in a rattling breath. 'I've got to go, my darling. I've got to pay my dues. I haven't been a good man.'

'Just wait a while.'

'You have your whole life ahead of you.'

He turned his unnaturally bright eyes away from me, looked straight ahead, and with a violent shudder, departed.

For a few seconds I simply stared at him. Appropriately, outside the October wind howled and dashed itself into the shutters. I knew the servants were waiting downstairs. Everyone was waiting for me to go down and tell them the news. Then I leaned forward and put my cheek on his still, bony chest. He smelled strongly of medicine. I closed my eyes tightly. Why did you have to go and die and leave me to the wolves?

In that moment I felt so close to him I wished that this time would not end. I wished I could lie on his chest, safe and closeted away from the cruel world. I heard the clock ticking. The flames in the fireplace crackled and spat. Somewhere a pipe creaked. I placed my chin on his chest and turned to look at him one last time. He appeared to be sleeping. Peaceful at any rate. I stroked the thin strands of white hair lying across his pinkish white scalp, and let my finger run down his prominent nose. It shocked me how quickly the tip of his nose had lost warmth. Soon all of him would be stone cold.

I wondered whom he had seen at the window. Who had come to take him to his reckoning. My sorrow was complete. I could put my fingertips into it and feel the edges. Smooth. Without corners. Without sharpness. It had no tears. I knew he was dying two hours before. Strange because it had seemed as if he had taken a turn for the better. He seemed stronger, his cheeks pink, his eyes brilliantly bright and when he smiled it appeared as if he was lit from within. He even looked so much stronger. I asked him what he wanted to eat.

'Milk. I'll have a glass of milk,' he said decisively.

But after I called for milk and it was brought to him he smiled and refused it. 'Isn't this wonderful?' he asked. 'I feel so good.'

And at that moment I knew. Even so it was incomprehensible to me that he was really gone. I never wanted to believe it.

'In the end you wanted to go, didn't you?'

 282

There was no answer.

'It's OK. I know you were tired. It was only me holding you back. You go on ahead. Find a place for me.'

He lay as still as a corpse. Oh God! I already missed him so much.

'I understand you can't talk. But you can hear me. When it is my turn I want you to come and get me. I'll be expecting you to come in through the window. Go in peace now, my love. All will be well. They will never know the truth. I will never tell them. To the day you come back to collect me.'

And then I began to cry, not loud, ugly sobs, but a quiet weeping. I didn't want the servants to hear. To come rushing in. Call the doctor waiting downstairs to come in and pronounce him dead. I knew what waited for me outside this room. Another hour...or two wouldn't make a difference. This was my time. My final hours with my husband.

The time before I became the hated gold digger.

35748767R00169

Printed in Great Britain
by Amazon